FLAMES OF THE BARE BROWN PASTURES

First Published in 2021

Beyond The Vale Publishing

Mandisa Hadebe

FLAMES OF THE BARE BROWN PASTURES

I dedicate this book to my late father, Sibongiseni Robert Hadebe.

Contents

1 – CRUMBS OF YOU

He knows that hair spray like he knows himself, seven years have passed, but it was still the same... Nandi had not changed at all, she was still that same slim, dark and tall girl he had last seen 7 years ago, on the day they went to fetch their Grade 12 statements in their old school - except now she was a woman.

***

She was not very happy when she realized that she had gotten six distinctions. Geography was not best friends with her, at least she had managed to pass it with a B. She had aimed at getting all seven for the subjects she was doing. She had wanted to make her mother proud, who was a principal at the nearby primary school where they lived, and she had succeeded in doing so. Mrs. Mazibuko was a widow. Her husband had died in his sleep three months after their wedding. She died with him that very morning; she had never been herself ever since that very morning. Seventeen years later, and not a day had ever passed by without her thinking about her late husband. Bheki was an attorney at a nearby law firm. Joyce was still a teacher back then. As usual, she had woken up first to prepare breakfast and their lunch boxes and prepare a bath for her husband.

When she went to wake him up, she realized that he was lifeless...

She regarded herself as one of the strongest women alive, for she had survived, especially on that day of her beloved husband's death, with her head high and her chest out. She had seen better days. They had not had any children yet, and so that was partly why she decided to adopt Nandipha, after her one-year mourning period following the death of her husband. Nandi was only 2 years old at that time. After the death of her husband, Mrs. Mazibuko had no relationship with her in-laws. They had never liked her, and so when their son died, they saw no need to have any contact with her. Joyce had no problems with that. She had expected that to happen because she knew that the family never liked her and had long accepted that. They always said that she is too proud, and she was full of herself. They also accused her of using a love portion on their son because she wanted to steal him from them. Bheki's younger sister had tried to keep in touch, but they suddenly stopped contacting each other. At least, unlike all Bheki's family members, she did not hate Joyce. She had always tried telling all the other family members that, if only they gave Joyce a chance, they could see that she was not at all a bad person. No one ever bothered to listen. Everyone had already drawn their conclusions. She let them all be and signed that she was never going to convince them anymore. Joyce knew and truly appreciated that, and it was enough. The communication was just going to be a bonus if it had not suddenly ceased.

Joyce's was a lonely life and she decided to focus her attention on her daughter. She had loved Bheki very much - she still did - and he was the only man she ever knew in her life, they dated when she was 15 years old and he was 17 years old.

They got married 16 years later when she was 31 years old. They had agreed that they should have children only after they got married. They wanted to provide a stable home for their children. They wanted to be there for their children and to give them love. They did not want to build their love on children, but they wanted to be fully ready for the responsibility of being parents and to be hands-on. Unfortunately, the universe had other plans. When her husband died, she made a promise to herself that she was going to honour his memory and remain single for the rest of her life. This was not an easy decision, and she had prayed to God that He kills her feelings for the male species. She had managed to keep the promise she had made to herself. No other man had known her nakedness, except for her late husband.

The only mother Nandi ever knew was Mrs. Mazibuko. Her biological mother had signed her up for adoption the moment she gave birth to her, so she had been told. She had taught herself to appreciate every little thing she had at a young age. She did not want to dwell on thinking about her biological mother. She just wanted to focus on the positive things in her life. She did not want to be affected by a past which she was not even a part of. She knew life had a lot to offer and being negative was just going to drag her down. She loved Mrs. Mazibuko and the feeling was mutual. She felt grateful that at least her mother had not aborted or killed her, at least according to her, she had done the 'right thing'. She had allowed her a chance to life. That was the biggest blessing and gift that her biological mother had given her. She was grateful for that. In her mind, she always told herself that her mother probably had her reasons why she could not keep her. She chose to respect her choices and decisions even though she did not know the reasons behind them. One would not know that Mrs. Mazibuko was not her biological mother. Sometimes she even forgot that. Mrs. Mazibuko loved her too much. She was her role model and biggest inspiration. Nandi knew how important it was that she passed with flying colours. Besides making her mother proud, she wanted to study medicine when she finished school.

Passing her matric was a step closer to making her dream of becoming a doctor, a reality. She would always imagine herself in the white lab coat and in scrubs going around saving lives. She would sometimes look at herself in the mirror and pretend to have heard that she had saved a patient's life. She would smile even thinking of her whole life having such a smile. She knew it was something she was going to do. Something which she had to do. She believed that being a doctor was her calling and it was going to be that, more than just a mere profession. She knew that she was going to pass even before the results came. She had never struggled academically. She was one of those learners who are said to be gifted. The only thing she was worried about was how exactly she was going to pass. She hated Geography, and it hated her back so she was really scared of how she was going to pass it even though she had never told this to anyone.

Her mother was so happy when the results came and decided to buy her clothes, "in preparation for tertiary life." She always bought her clothes so that was just an excuse to spoil her more. "You passed with a bachelor, Nandi, with six distinctions and a B!" said her mother holding the newspaper in her hands with a smile on her face. "If I could, I would buy you the whole world. You have made me so proud, my baby." She knew she had made her proud. At least she had done something to make her proud.

Nandi and Thapelo went to the same school. Nandi started going to that school when she was doing grade 8. She was known as the "Dark Beauty" and almost every learner loved her. She was the girl everyone wished they could befriend. She was outgoing and talked to everyone. She was popular. She also passed well and that automatically worked to her advantage. Thapelo changed schools and came to that school when he was going to do his grade 10. His family had relocated because his father had found a job in that area. He was generally resistant to change. He was too down to earth and found it hard to socialize. He had spent almost all his time outside school at home sitting alone and writing pieces of work that he had a wish to one day publish. Sometimes he would play chess with his closest and best friend, Thami. He was his only friend. They would challenge each other and learn new tricks of chess. That was his favourite sport. He had not liked the idea of moving to a new place and enrolling in a new school, but he had no choice. He was going to be leaving his only friend behind and he did not like the idea of trying to make new friends all over again. His father had worked for a construction company and was retrenched with his other colleagues when the company had financial problems. He applied for UIF and would be paid all his money that was due. He knew that, with no money coming in, they should soon become bankrupt, so he had to find a job. His mother had worked as a cleaner in one of the clinics nearby. She had not earned much, but she had been satisfied with what she did, and she could help in paying bills around the house.

Thapelo's father - Mr. Zondi - got a job as a janitor in a firm for which he had applied for. His prayers had been answered. They were all forced to relocate. Mrs. Zondi was not happy that she was going to leave her job, but she had no choice. When they had settled in their new home, she started looking for a job and got one in a salon, doing general work. Life was manageable. Thapelo's two siblings were also enrolled at the primary school where Mrs. Mazibuko was principal. Thapelo, being an introvert did not help him, was not so enthusiastic about the new school, but he had no other choice. When he went to school, he was placed into the class where Nandi was. She was a prefect and an additional member of the RCL. Even though Thapelo had realized then that he had feelings for her, he knew he did not stand a chance. Nandi was popular and the teachers loved her. He, on the other hand, was just this "new boy" who had arrived. The boy struggled even to make friends and spent almost all his breaktime stuck or hiding, as some of his classmates put it, in his class. Nandi had always wished to take him out of his shell, to say something, to befriend him, but she just never knew where to start, so she let it go.

Nandi had never forgotten the first day she saw Thapelo. It was his first day at school and he had come with his mother. Her teacher had sent her to make copies in the administration office. Seeing her, Thapelo felt a cold shiver consuming his whole body. That feeling was alien to him. He had never felt like that before. He wished to share the feeling with her if only he knew that she felt exactly the same way. Later that day when she described the boy he saw, she said, "The moment I saw him, I knew he was my soulmate." Her friends just laughed at her. It was a miracle that Thapelo went to the same class as her.

That year ended, and neither of them had shared their feelings with the other. Thapelo wanted to say something, but he was scared she was going to reject him. He had never felt like this about any girl before, neither had he had a girlfriend. He did not know what to expect, especially from someone as beautiful as Nandi. She waited in vain, that whole year, for him to make a move on her. She also had never had a boyfriend before, but with no doubt, she knew what she felt for Thapelo was love. She wanted him to tell her he loved her, she wanted to tell him she loved him back, but he never made that move in grade 10. She learnt to live with all the shivers she got whenever their eyes would meet, and all the feelings she thought she had for him. They both learnt to live without each other in one another's life, even though they both wished they could be together.

In the following year, he had loosened up. Even though he was still shy, at least he had gotten used to the environment. He had made some friends, and he no longer had as hard a time as before when he had to stand in front of his class for orals. Some things had changed, but not his feelings for Nandi. He was convinced that she was more beautiful with each day that passed by. He always stole glances at her, and every time he did, he made a promise to himself that one day when he was a teacher and a famous poet, writer, and novelist he was going to marry her. Not only that, he always hoped that one day he could write a novel, specifically about her. He truly loved her. One evening, before he went to sleep, he decided to write a letter to Nandi. He knew that with a letter it was going to be easy. He could pour out all his feelings and thoughts without any interruptions. At least he would not have to look at her or have her look at him. He also knew that she could have time to think about everything that he was going to write in that letter. With shaking hands, he started to write the letter:

"Nandipha,

I know I am the last person from which you would expect a letter. I also know that there is no reason why you should bother yourself and waste your time by reading this letter, but I should really appreciate it if you did.

Unfortunately, I do not have gold or diamonds to offer to you, but I believe, in fact I know, that if you could give me a chance, I could give you love. I know I am young, Nandi, and you also still are, but I love you and I am certain of that. Could you please be my girlfriend, Nandi? I promise I shall make you the happiest girl alive. I want to grow old with you. I love you, Nandipha Maluleka. If I could, I would promise you the Heavens and all of planet Earth, but I cannot do that because I know it is something which I cannot give you. I am promising to give you love because I know it is something which I can and am planning to give you. You are the most beautiful girl I have ever seen and yet you are so humble. Allow me to love you, please.

I am sure that as you will be reading this letter, you shall wonder why I did not come to you. To be honest, I loved you the first time I saw you last year, but I have always been scared that you would reject me. I could no longer hold my feelings for you, so I decided to write. If you feel the same, I should be very happy. If you do not, I know I should be hurt. Either way, at least I will have no regrets. Please forgive me for writing instead of coming to you.

Love,

Thapelo.

The following day, he slid the letter inside Nandi's bag during assembly. Nobody saw him do it. Nandi could not believe her eyes when she read the letter. She was so happy; she could not even hide it. After school, she told Thapelo that she had something to tell him. "I love you too, Thapelo," she suddenly said after they sat in one of the classes so they could talk.

Thapelo had never understood from where he had taken so much courage, but just then he kissed her. She did not resist. It was both their first kiss and it had so much passion with uncertainty from both sides, neither of them wanted to do the wrong thing. Thapelo complimented on how she smelt. He loved the way her hair smelt. "Thank you," she said shyly. They were both happy and started talking and getting to know one another better. They talked about their families, both their childhoods and a lot of other things. Going to their homes, they held hands. The teenagers were happy that they had found each other and Thapelo was secretly thanking and praising himself for writing the letter.

The typical Sagittarius, Nandi had no plans of getting married in her life, at least not after she had met her typical Virgo Thapelo. If someone had to sneak and eavesdrop on their conversations, they would need more convincing that the people who were talking were only teenagers. Their talks were usually serious and about both their futures. Nandi wanted to study medicine and travel the world with her own money. Thapelo advised her that she should consider modelling, at least part-time, but she was not interested. A lot of people had advised her about it but she only wanted to focus on medicine. She did not want to have children, nor did she want to get married, at least not until she reached 35 years. She just wanted to have freedom and travel the world with her mother. She did not want to have any commitments to hold her from grabbing any opportunities which might come her way. She had planned on having children with the person she was going to settle down with when she was sure she could be capable to take care of them, to be a mother and a wife. She had planned to live a carefree life and enjoy every moment of her life in every way she could. However, some of those plans changed when Thapelo came into her life.

Thapelo wanted to study B. Ed and change lives. Even though he was not very much interested in teaching, his wish was to be an agent of change. His biggest passion was writing. His biggest wish was to publish his own novel one day, or some of the work he had already written, which was mostly poetry. He was certain that he was going to get married and had planned to have two children. He had planned to settle early in his life and focus on his family, his career and his talent, writing. He was now certain that the woman he was going to marry and settle down with was Nandi. He had no doubts about that. He was too introverted to have any travelling plans in his future life which he had in his mind. Hearing his plans, Nandi decided that she should allow Thapelo to marry her and carry his children, maybe they could travel later in life. She was happy to have him in her life and the feeling was mutual. Thapelo also promised that he was going to travel with her and go against his introverted self. They were genuinely happy.

In grade 12 they both agreed to give each other enough time to study and not be too clingy. This was Thapelo's suggestion, "If we want to pass, if you want to go and study medicine next year, then we shall have to cut our time together." Nandi agreed. They sometimes met so that Nandi could help Thapelo with some mathematics practice and they made sure not to play around, they wanted to pass, and they knew that it came with a price. They were happy and wanted nothing more than their future plans and dreams to become reality. Nandi had promised that she was going to be there when Thapelo published his first book, and she had promised that she would support him fully. They became best friends and they were like siblings. They were both truly in love. During their final exams, they only saw each other at school. They did not call each other every time or text like they did in the middle of the year.

Results came in January, and they had both passed. Thapelo had also passed with a bachelor's pass and had managed to get two distinctions. He was going to study B. Ed at the University of KwaZulu-Natal, Edgewood Campus. They were truly happy. That evening, Thapelo invited Nandi to his house. His parents had gone to a family ceremony which was out of town. That afternoon they took each other's virginity. Nandi had gotten a bursary to study medicine in Cuba. Her mother refused to let her go alone. She loved her too much to let her go into a new country alone. She had already planned to retire so she planned to use her savings and go with her daughter. She was going to relocate, and once Nandi had gotten her degree, it would be up to her to decide where she wanted to live. Thapelo listened carefully as Nandi explained while he accompanied her to her home. "So, everything has been finalized?"

"Yes, baby. We are leaving early tomorrow. Mom has sorted everything out." she answered. That slightly broke Thapelo's heart, but he was happy for her. She was excited that she was going to a new place and to start a new life, she lived for adventure, but she was sad that she was going to leave her Thapelo behind.

"But what about us Nandi? Do you think we are going to survive this? We are going to be in two different countries. Does our relationship, all our plans and dreams, does all that stand a chance?"

"On my side, I promise to try my best, Thapelo. I promise to give it my all. Are you willing to put in the effort?"

"Of course, I am willing, Nandipha. I love you. I would do anything for us to work, sweetheart. I want to marry you one day."

"We shall call each other every day, text, video call and keep the communication going."

"Do you promise, Nandi?" Thapelo asked looking directly and straight into her eyes.

"I promise. Thapelo. Do you also promise that we shall communicate daily?"

"I promise, Nandi. I promise." They then hugged each other, tightly. He smelt the lavender scent which her hair breathed, and which he loved so much. It was as though they were holding each other for dear life so that life could not separate them.

His voice was cracking but he managed to whisper, "I love you," and she managed to whisper it back, as she closed her eyes tightly.

They then separated, promising to keep in touch. Nandi went and found her mother packing their clothes. Mrs. Mazibuko had started packing days before, so it was not much that was left. She helped her, but she was dying inside. She could not wait to go to her room and cry. She was hurt that she was going to leave Thapelo. She promised herself that she was going to do everything for them to work. When he arrived at his home, Thapelo cried and slept for the whole afternoon to wake up the next morning. He texted her asking if she had left and she said she was at the airport waiting for their flight with her mother. He was breaking. He spent that whole day in bed, he was broken, and his heart was hurt. They both shared the same pain. That was when they had last seen each other.

***

He knows that hairspray like he knows himself. He turns to look at the person who has just patted him on his shoulder. That hair spray brings in his mind memories that he had long tried to forget in his life. It awakens sleeping emotions which he had learnt to bury in his heart. He turns. Even though his mind had alerted him of what/who he was about to see because of the smell of the hair spray shampoo, but his eyes could not believe it. There she stood, still the same slim, dark and tall woman. She has grown and is more beautiful, he thinks to himself.

"You act as though you have seen a ghost," she says smiling.

"Hello, Nandi," he finally says.

It all comes back to him. The wasted years, the long nights of prayers that went unanswered, the hurt. It all comes back to him, then and there. Back in grades 11 and 12, they could understand everything another said, just by looking into another's eyes. Nandi looks at Thapelo. To her surprise, she could still hear everything he was saying just by looking at his eyes. She feels her own eyes getting wet. She thinks of all the broken promises, all the love which has gone wasted in the past years. She realizes all over again how broken she is. Thapelo also can understand everything that runs through her mind. They are both at a loss for words. They both have a lot they want to say, but somehow, they are not able to utter anything.

She sees the ring. It shines as though to make its presence be felt.

"Congratulations," she says quietly, almost to herself. He knows what she is talking about.

"Thanks," he says showing indifference.

For some reason, she feels the need to blink rapidly. He realizes that and looks sideways, avoiding eye contact. He does not look at her fingers, but something tells him that her fingers have no symbol of commitment to someone. He feels a sharp pain in his heart, sudden. He feels like he has betrayed her. This is something he has never thought about before, until now. He has never imagined himself in this kind of position before, neither has he ever thought about this moment. All the promises come back to haunt him. The promise he made 7 years ago, saying that he was going to marry her. He had married someone else and not her. He looks at her and realizes that she is looking straight into his eyes.

"It's okay," she says. "I understand."

He nods as though to say he appreciates her understanding and hopes that she does not hate him. Words keep on failing him. If only he had a pen and a paper, he could be able to write down all the emotions which crowded his heart, uninvited, and unannounced.

"Thank you," he manages to say.

"I'm sorry," they both say simultaneously. They both keep quiet and laugh. At least they can laugh now. That is progress. They laugh until both their eyes fill up with tears. Their stomachs start to feel sore. Their laughter is filled with sorrow and sadness. It has regrets. They laugh. They laugh. They laugh. Nandi contains herself. She rummages around into her handbag and takes out an envelope. She gives it to Thapelo, and he opens it without asking what is inside. He takes out the small piece of paper. It is the letter which he wrote for her 8 years ago, in grade 11.

"You kept it all these years?" he asks the obvious.

"I read it every time it all got too much. It is the only thing I have been holding on to, although it no longer has your smell, but just to have it is enough."

"Then why are you giving it to me. It is yours."

"I need to move on, Thapelo. It is my constant reminder not to forget and I need not be reminded anymore. It is what I had when I felt I was losing the little crumbs of you I was in possession of. I have lost you and I believe there is no need why I should hold on to it anymore. If you are not going to take it, then I am going to be forced to burn or throw it away."

"So there has never been anyone else after you left?"

"No," she says plainly, showing no emotion.

***

When Nandi arrived in Cuba, she was neutral. She did not know how to react. She missed Thapelo and felt guilty that she had left him. They talked every day with Thapelo and everything was promising that indeed they should work out. For someone like Nandi, it was surprising that she struggled to fit in at the new place. Her mother was there for her and she showered her with all the love, but she still struggled. The new life, the school, meeting new people, missing Thapelo, it all got too much for her. She started isolating herself from everyone and withdrew from social media. She even hated her own cellphone. Three months after they had settled, she was diagnosed with depression. Her mother had never stopped trying to make her better. She needed Thapelo but she did not know if he was going to understand how she felt. She hated everyone and had anger issues; everything had changed. She was not the same Nandi Thapelo had last seen. Thapelo tried his best to keep his promise, to keep the communication between them going. Nandi too tried her best. She needed him more than ever. He did not know what to say or do but he assured her that he was there. She started treatment and got better.

Thapelo and Nandi drifted away from each other. The phone calls, texts and chatting on social media started to change. They both felt like they were losing another and the effort from both sides was reduced. They both had to focus on their studies. They both felt lost and out of place, varsity life was different from what they knew as normal. They could both feel that they were losing each other, but the interest from both sides seemed to have been lost. The love was there, but something was missing. Both yearned physical touches. For the past two years, they had been living in the same town and going to the same school. They saw each other almost every day. This new life both had to adapt to was not as easy as they had initially thought. They did not even know when they were going to see each other.

Thapelo lost his mother in the following year when they were both doing their second year. It was just two days after his birthday, on August the 25th. He was so desperate to get her phone call. She had not even called to wish him a happy birthday nor write just a simple text, so he had no hopes of ever hearing from her again. He needed her to call. To tell her how he felt like he told all the poetry he wrote every night before he went to sleep. To hear her voice, to hear her assure him that this was not the end of the world. He never got that call. She was still recovering from her depression and he had just fallen into his own. The two waited in vain for each to communicate to another.

Around the same time, Thapelo's birthday, Nandi fell into depression again. She pushed everyone who cared about her away. She was a walking ghost of the girl she once was. Everything was too much. The phone calls between her and Thapelo had already ceased. Each one of them waited for the other to call. Thapelo did not even know that Nandi had fallen into depression again. She felt she had done all that she had come to do in life. She could no longer continue. On her birthday, early December, she tried to commit suicide. When Thapelo called to wish her a happy birthday, it just rang, and his call was never picked. He was hurt. She had not even wished him one on his birthday in August. He was hurt then, but he was more hurt when she did not pick up his call on her own birthday. That time, she was lying in bed fighting for her life, the same life she had tried to take. At that very moment, she needed him and his soft warm hands to hold hers. She needed just his hug, even though the state she was in was not going to allow her to return it, but she needed it. Mrs. Mazibuko never stopped supporting her. She got better just before schools opened in the year that followed. It was a miracle that she had passed the previous year. A lot had happened

In both their third years, Thapelo had given up the waiting game, hoping that things would ever get better. Nandi was still hoping that perhaps things could still go back to normal. She decided to give it a try and called one evening in late October, the day that Thapelo was going to spend the night with Nomkhosi. He had gone to the bathroom and requested that Nomkhosi answer the call for him if it was not his father. Nandi's contacts were no longer saved in Thapelo's cellphone. Even if they still were, she had changed her number. When Nomkhosi answered the call, Nandi's whole body froze. She just dropped the call and never called again. Thapelo asked who had called and Nomkhosi told him that the person just kept quiet and dropped so she did not know who it was. "It must be a wrong number then," he said. He had moved on, Nandi concluded. She decided she was not going to focus on relationships and decided that she was going to focus on her life, school and making her mother proud. She had already put her through a lot. They never spoke again with Thapelo.

***

"When I tried calling on your birthday, in our second year, and you did not pick up, I was convinced you had moved on."

"I was in hospital. I stayed there for almost two months."

He quickly looks up at her and looks her up and down, as though by doing so he was going to see what had been wrong with her. "What was wrong, Nandi? What had happened? Are you okay now?"

She does not reply immediately. She seems doubtful as to whether she should reply. The worry on his face tells her anyway. She almost regrets bringing this up in the first place.

"Nandi," he says looking at her, forcing her to look back at him. She knows he will not stop asking, not until she speaks up.

"Please do not judge me, Thape..."

"You know I could never do that. A lot may have happened, but I am still the same man you fell in love with years ago. I had never judged you for anything before and I am not about to start now."

"I know. I am sorry. I had tried to commit suicide, Thapelo," she says quickly, as though she was afraid that she would change her mind before actually saying it.

"I understand. And I am so sorry, Nandi. Are you okay now though?"

"Come on, Thapelo. It has been years now since that happened. I am okay now, thanks. I am a lot better."

"I am so relieved to hear that. I am."

"I thought of you every day. Every single day," she says, not allowing him to finish his sentence. "I had always had hope that one day I should wake up to find your text. I never lost hope. I remember calling you and a girl answered this one evening during both our third years. I realized you had moved on and I gave up. I was hurt but I hoped that at least you were happy."

"I am sorry, Nandi. For everything."

"It's okay, Thapelo."

"When I called on your birthday, I just found an excuse, your birthday. My mother had died. Two days after my birthday."

"August the 25th," she says quietly.

He pauses to look at her. He is surprised that after all these years she still remembers his birthday, but then again, he still remembers hers also. "I needed you, Nandi. I needed my best friend. Someone whom I knew would understand every little pain I felt. Knowing you cared would have been consolation enough" he continues. "I had never felt so much pain before. I needed you more than ever. I waited for your call in vain."

"I am so sorry, Thapelo. My deepest condolences. I am so sorry I couldn't be there for you when you needed me most."

"Such is life. It's okay."

"Do you still write?" she asks. He had not expected that question.

"I try." He does not know if he should tell her about the novel he wrote. He decides to say nothing more than what he had already said. Nandi realizes that he does not want to talk about it, judging by his response. She understands and asks no more. They look into each other's eyes without saying a word. They are both lost in another's eyes. Each gets lost in their own thoughts.

"Love, I am back. Are you still okay?" asks Khosi looking at Thapelo.

***

Thapelo had met Nomkhosi when he was doing his second year in varsity. His mother had just died of natural causes, she felt ill and her body could not take it anymore. They were approaching exams. Thapelo was in despair and needed Nandi. He needed her support, her hug, to smell her, he needed her to just listen to him, even without necessarily saying anything. He needed his best friend. He felt so empty and lost. Nomkhosi was a first-year student then. They had met at the library and they started chatting. The two were comfortable around each other. Thapelo got someone on whom he could unload. Someone who reminded him that things were not going to stay that way forever. Slowly, Thapelo was getting better and was getting used to the reality that he was motherless.

He liked Nomkhosi, but he did not ask her out that year. He did not want to sabotage their friendship. Besides, he did not want to hurt her in case Nandi came back into his life. Nomkhosi was too kind and honest and would not deserve so much hurt. She had already been through a lot. They decided to be friends. Nomkhosi told him that she was still healing from her first heartbreak. Her boyfriend had cheated on her with her best friend and she was still trying to get over that. Thapelo too had still not let go of Nandi. When he called her on her birthday and she did not answer he was disappointed, but the fact that he still loved her had not changed. He had hopes that perhaps she was still going to come back into his life, and they could fix things. He loved her too much.

In the year that followed, when he was doing his third year, he started to lose hope. He saw the last pieces of Nandi that he had been in possession of disappearing in his eyes. He started feeling more hurt and finally accepted that she was not going to come back. He gave up waiting. After he was convinced that he had healed, he started pursuing Nomkhosi. She was single, towards the end of the first semester that year, they were an item.

As soon as he finished his degree, he paid lobola for Nomkhosi. After she had also gotten her degree, they got married. In the year that followed, they were blessed with a son. He was a year and a few months old now. Thapelo never stopped writing. When he was doing his first year, he started writing a novel about Nandi. He had planned to give it to her to read when they saw each other. As their relationship started to fall and finally failed, he never finished the novel. Whenever he would miss her too much, he would read the few chapters he had written. Ever since Nomkhosi became a part of his life, he never read the novel again, neither did he ever try to continue writing or editing it, but he did not delete it. They cared for each other, Nomkhosi and he. Their relationship was built on trust, honesty, respect and communication. He wanted to be a loving husband to her and a responsible father to his children. Nomkhosi was grateful for meeting him in her life. She considered him as the biggest blessing in her life and their son. Thapelo was her biggest support system. He was her pillar.

Nomkhosi was not the complete opposite of Nandi. She was also dark but not like Nandi, but she was not so slim, she was chubby. She was short. She had a heart of gold. That is one of the things which had attracted Thapelo to her, she was kind and usually put others before her. She could not even hurt a fly. She cared about everyone and she spread love wherever she was. She was a true "goddess", as Thapelo would sometimes refer to her. When they first met, Thapelo was afraid that he was going to hurt her. That was his biggest fear. He would hate himself if he ever did something to break her heart. She had been a true friend to him. When he had lost his mother, it was towards exams and it was difficult for him. They had known each other for a short period, but she was always there for him. He would call her every time it got too much, and by the time he would have to drop the call, he would be feeling fine, light. Even the time when he told her about Nandi, she was so understanding, and she was the reason he kept going. He had always cursed her previous boyfriend for hurting her. He did not understand how he slept at night after breaking Khosi's heart. He despised him. He wanted to treat her right and make her happy. She respected him and that was the least she could do, and it was enough for Thapelo. The foundation of their relationship was strong, and it had helped them to go through everything that they had been through and move on still strong. Nomkhosi always had a smile on her face. She was simply kind and beautiful inside and out.

***

Thapelo does not reply. He is not sure if he is okay or not. He looks at Nomkhosi. She is not the same Nomkhosi who is always smiling or slightly laughing. She looks pale, he cannot tell what she is feeling. She looks at Nandi, and with no doubt, she knows this is the Nandi she had been told about. "Hello," she says to her. She cannot hear Nandi mumbling her own "Hello" because she is still surprised by the way Thapelo is

30

looking at her. She has never seen Thapelo looking at any woman, not even her, like this.

Thapelo and Khosi had come to buy a few things because they were visiting Nomkhosi's mother. They were then going to take their son Siphosethu with them because he had visited his grandmother after she had complained about missing her grandson. Thapelo did not like going into a store with Nomkhosi because she was naturally slow. And she hated him always hurrying her up, for no particular reason sometimes. Almost every time they would go together, they would leave the store angry at each other, or not on speaking terms. So, he had realized that the only way to keep the peace was if she went inside the store and he waited outside. It worked for both parties.

"Khosi, this is Nandipha. Nandi, this is Nomkhosi," Thapelo says as he looks at Nandi. He does not think he has to describe either of them to another.

"I am happy to meet you," Nandi says as she extends her right hand for a shake.

"Likewise," Khosi says with a smile on her face, as they shake hands. She is a little at ease now. This had first taken her by surprise.

Thapelo cannot help but feel relieved. He had not known how this was going to turn out.

"It was nice seeing you, Thapelo. Keep well," she says. "Khosi, you are very lucky. I hope you know that. Please take care of him. You also take care," she says as she turns to look at Nomkhosi.

"Will do. Thank you. You also take care," she answers still smiling.

Nandi turns and leaves the couple standing. Thapelo's eyes are still glued on her until she turns the corner. Nomkhosi keeps quiet and pretends to not have seen that.

"She is beautiful," she says.

"She has not changed."

"Let us go before we lose track of time, love." They leave.

In the car, they do not talk. The only thing which is trying to communicate to them is the music which is playing. It is Thapelo's favourite, deep house. As he is driving, he is travelling to places with his mind. Nomkhosi too is thinking about what had just happened. Maybe the two still love each other, she thinks to herself, but what does that mean for her marriage with Thapelo? The way he kept looking at her does not leave her mind. She knows Thapelo too well and she could see, just, by the way, he looked at Nandi that, he is crazy about her. With no doubt, Thapelo still loves Nandi, she concludes as she thinks to herself. Thapelo is taken back to grade 11. He is thinking about the last day they saw each other when they both lost their virginity. He is taken back to the present by cars hooting at him. The robot has just turned red and he had not realized it. The other drivers are furious and are swearing at him. He apologizes and continues driving. Nomkhosi sees this but decides to keep quiet. If Thapelo sees the need to talk to her about what happened, she is going to wait for him and not ask anything. Upon arriving at Nomkhosi's home, the two get out of the car to go inside. Thapelo takes the bags, which they had arrived with, from the car and brings them inside the house. Khosi's mother comes to greet them in the dining with a sleeping Siphosethu on her back. She had already prepared food for them and tells her daughter to dish up. They eat while engaging in small talk, about work and the weather and other not so important things. Nomkhosi's mother cannot help but feel that something is going on between her daughter and her son in law, but she says nothing about it. After eating, she thanks them for the things which they had brought and gives them a bag full of Siphosethu's clothes and his essentials. Thapelo thanks her mother-in-law for a delicious late lunch. Nomkhosi carefully takes the baby from her mother. "Do not underestimate the power of prayer my child. Never stop praying. I will do the same here," her mother says to her as she turns and is about to head to the car. She turns back to look at her mother. "Thank you," she says with a forced smile and leaves. She arrives and gets in the car. They leave.

It suddenly feels like there is a wall that has been built between Thapelo and Khosi. In the car, Siphosethu is still sleeping, nobody says anything. This worries Khosi because ever since they knew each other, they have always talked about things. The transparency in their relationship was not just a fancy word which they used, they were always honest and talked about anything with each other. This worries her now, but she is not about to cry. No, she is not going to cry. Not while they are on the road. The mind says one thing, but the heart says another. Her heartbreaks, then and there. Everything that they have been through with Thapelo comes to her mind, all the memories that they have made in the years which they have been together. Neither of them had ever cheated before and that is why they trusted each other this much, she thinks. But how does one deal with something like this? How do you compete with someone like Nandi, Thapelo's first love? Someone with whom he shared so many memories. They never even ended things between each other. The gates of her eyes open and the tears slowly flow. Thapelo looks at her and his own heartbreaks. He knows exactly what is happening. He knows he has done wrong by her and feels horrible about it.

Luckily, they have arrived. He parks just as they get into the gate and goes to open the door for her. Always, she'd put Siphosethu in the backseat whenever he went with them. She knows the rules and never made any mistakes, but she is still holding him now. Thapelo whispers to her that he is coming back just now and takes the sleeping Siphosethu to put him to sleep in the bedroom. He quickly comes back and opens the door again. He takes his wife's hand and helps her get out of the car. He then engulfs her into his arms. They hug each other for a long time. This makes Khosi cry even more.

"I am so sorry, Nomkhosi," he says quietly while he brushes her back. He knows this always calms her down. However, it does not seem to work today. She moves out of his arms and goes to sleep in the guestroom. Thapelo follows her to go to the study. He misses his computer. He feels the need to write. He does not want to interrupt her. Every time Nomkhosi feels down, sleeping calms her. She only takes her coat and shoes off and sleeps with the clothes she is wearing. She quickly falls asleep. Thapelo hears his son cry in their bedroom and he attends to him rather than waking his mother. He changes his nappy and feeds him his porridge. He then gives him his toys and looks at him while he plays. He realizes how lucky he is. He wants to wake Nomkhosi up and thank her for giving him the best gift in his whole life, Siphosethu. He looks at his son playing and realizes that he would never trade him or Nomkhosi for anything or anyone. They have made him the man he is, and he would never have chosen anything else. He then baths his son and puts him on their bed with Nomkhosi. He plays with his toys and finally falls asleep again. He remembers that he had planned to write something. It has been years since he tried to scribble his thoughts. He had even given up on the novel he had promised Nandi that he was going to publish. He goes to the study to take his laptop and comes back with it.

He had planned to write something, but he soon finds himself scrolling down in the unfinished novel he had written about Nandi. He never deleted it. Just when he is about to read it, he is interrupted by a text which he gets. He does not recognize the number.

"*I was not sure if you would get this message, because I was not sure if you still use the same number. Your conservative nature made me believe that you still do. I hope you do. It was nice seeing you. I must say you have not changed. You have always been true to yourself. I am happy for you, Thapelo. You deserve all the happiness in the world. I am glad I saw you, finally, I can move on. I guess perhaps, I needed closure. You are an amazing man, Thapelo. You are very special. I hope you treat her right; she deserves it. I could tell she is also an amazing woman. I wish you both all the best in your marriage and that comes from a good place. I shall be leaving tonight. I want to travel the world, enjoy seeing nature and meet new people. I also do modelling now, part-time, yup! I do not think we shall ever see each other again. I will block and delete your contacts as soon as this message sends. I believe that is for the best. Take care, Nandipha.*"

He does not know why, but his heart breaks. He knows he is happy for her. She has always wanted to travel the world and take every opportunity thrown her way. He suddenly feels proud of her. Especially because she did consider modelling. He thinks about what she said that she had never fallen in love with anyone else after him. He thinks that there is no point in him replying since Nandi probably has already blocked and deleted his contacts. He reads the text message at least five times before he finally puts the cellphone away. He begins to read the novel again, silently. He gets lost in it. He had written about the first day he saw her. She was so beautiful; he had described it. He had also written about the whole year when they were doing grade 10, how he was afraid to approach her because he was scared, she would reject him. He had also written about the day he wrote that letter, one evening, in grade 11. He pauses as he remembers that she gave him the letter earlier. He searches his pockets and finds it. He does not read it, instead, he tears it up and leaves its pieces scattered on the table.

He continues reading the novel. He had written about the love they shared in grades 11 and 12. As he reads, he realizes that he misses it, the love they shared. He continues to read until the part where he had written about the last day they saw each other and the promises they made to one another. He does not want to read anymore. He is torturing himself; he realizes. He quickly deletes the novel and feels a lump in his throat. He swallows. He is proud of himself for deleting the novel. He is not the only one who has been holding on, he thinks to himself. He has erased every piece there was in his life of his first love. He has gotten rid of whatever crumbs of her there still were in his life. Even though he feels slightly sad, he knows he has done the right thing. "Goodbye, Nandi," he mumbles to himself as he continues sitting on that chair, hopelessly, staring at the computer screen.

Nomkhosi comes and stands at the door of their bedroom and he does not realize she has come. The last time she had seen him like this, glued to his laptop was when his mother died when he was doing his second year. They were not an item then, but she learnt then that writing helps him, whenever he is feeling down. She looks at him and thinks about the wonderful man he had been all the years to her and how he has always been there for her and Siphosethu. She realizes that she loves him, and she would not be where she is if it was not for him. She wishes that they could talk about what is happening like they always do. She wants him to pour his feelings into her like he always does. She knows, deep in her heart that Thapelo still loves Nandi. She just does not know where that puts her. She remembers how he would sometimes tell her that she has gained weight, politely though. She does not want to entertain the thought that perhaps, Thapelo only pursued her because he was hoping that she would replace Nandi. She realizes how that could break her if it...

"Love," he says interrupting her thoughts. She did not realize when Thapelo turned and looked at her. "Could we please talk?"

"I still need to bath Siphosethu, feed him and put him to sleep. It is late now," she says.

"I have already done that. He has just fallen asleep while he was playing on our bed."

"Thank you," she says briefly. Silence suddenly sinks the room. "Do you still love her?" she is surprised at herself that she has asked that. Her mouth just spoke without consulting her mind. Thapelo is happy that she has asked. He had no idea how he was going to bring it up.

"When I saw her, something inside of me shook. Something old, and very strong. We were once an item, Khosi, and I obviously still care about her, especially because we never fought. The way everything happened does not make things easier for any of us. She will always be a part of my past, sweetheart. I will always appreciate the time I spent with her, but that does not mean I love her. She was obviously my first love and that shall never change. I love you, Nomkhosi, and no other woman."

"When you pursued me, were you in any way hoping that I could replace her?"

"Why would you even think that, love?"

"You sometimes told me that I have gained and put pressure on me that I should lose some…"

"No, Khosi. I could never do something like that to you. Before I pursued you, I made sure that I had healed. I could never do something so selfish. I love you, sweetheart. I love you so much, Nomkhosi. Nandi is a part of my past, and you are my present and future. I was not aware that I would bump into her today, and when I did, I honestly did not know how to react. Please never think like that again. You know I am crazy about your body. You are enough, sweetheart, in every way, for me."

"Please, hug me," she says softly. He comes close to her and he holds her tightly.

"I love you," he whispers in her right ear as he hugs her.

"I love you too," she manages to say as tears make their way from her eyes, wetting his warm bare neck. They remain in each other's embrace, hoping that this does not create a permanent dent in their marriage. She chooses not to think about the way he looked at her. She wants to enjoy this, the hug and the moment. She wants to forget whatever happened today and enjoy the warmth of her husband. She wants to think about nothing, except for the love which she feels for this man who is holding her so tight. She feels secure and for that moment, she hopes that nothing would ever take this away from her. Today had made her realize that, if she lost Thapelo, she would not survive.

He thinks that he has lost his one and only first love, for the second time. He feels himself holding her tight as if to say, "Do not leave me too."

2 – US, WE

We went to the river early in the morning for water and sometimes to the forest to fetch wood. Ours was just a small village that did not even have electricity. We were just like one big happy family. The school was far and a lot of us, the female species, did not even bother to go to school because it was generally believed that we were going to get married and bear children for our husbands. A lot of us had no problem with that because even our mothers had grown up that way, so we were bound to follow the same route. However, some of us did not believe in that. They wanted to get educated and become 'independent' in case things did not go as planned, so they would say. That was not a problem. Nobody stood in their way.

We led a simple life. We would go and plant crops in our gardens and hardly went to buy anything in the shop. Every year there would be a ceremony whereby girls and young women who are still virgins would sing traditional songs and dance. That was my favourite time of the year and activity. I always went every year, perhaps with hopes to find myself a man who could marry and take care of me. The young men who would be ready to get married should choose from the young women and after some time they would get married. Growing up in that community was life. We did not lead luxurious lives, but I would not have traded my life for anything. Everyone cared for each other like their own. We were all happy.

Bongani was one of us. He was my neighbour and we went to the same school. His father was famous for his herbs because he was a traditional doctor. Bongani was one of the handsome young men in our village. I have heard people talking about perfect beauty, especially in females. I would be lying if I said Bongani was that 'perfect beauty' kind of handsome. He was not ugly neither. But there was something about him. Something which got every girl excited and hope that she would get a chance to know him better. Now let me give you a picture of what he looked like. He was dark in complexion, almost black, like a blackberry.

He was tall and had a body that I believe every guy would be happy to own. He walked as though the grounds he walked on would crack. His body was firm and seemed strong. His eyes were slightly big and round, straight nose and thin lips which were very noticeable because his white teeth were protruding, forcing the lips and his upper jaw to do the same. He was naturally a gentleman. He went to school until he finished his matric. He was every girl's dream in our village. Everyone spoke of him. He was the guy to whom parents wished their daughter would get married. He did not pursue anyone until he went to university. He was the first one to go to university in our community. Others would only obtain their matric certificates and that would be it. He was determined to go the extra mile. We were all happy for him. By the time he finished his matric, I had already been engaged and expecting and was just going to get married soon. We bid our goodbyes and wished him well.

We heard that he was going to study civil engineering, something which a lot of us had little or no information about.

That was not important. Everyone was just happy that one of us was to know the gates of a university. His father organised an ancestral farewell ceremony for him. He was happy, and so were all of us were. We were all proud of him.

Personally, my life was not something that I had always dreamt of, especially after marriage. I just changed families and was warmly accepted in my new family. My husband did not stay at home. He was working like most of the other married men in our community. He had found work in the farms which were not nearby our homes, and so he could not stay at home. That is not something upon which we had agreed before marriage. He had promised that he was going to spend as much time at home as possible. When I asked him why I could not go with him to the farms he would say that he did not have a stable house and he did not want to make me stay in an unfavourable place.

Moving on, he ended up only coming back home once a month. The fact that I was pregnant meant nothing to him. He was not willing to change. After giving birth, life was hard because he had stopped sending money home. That forced me to go look for work. I would do washing for my neighbours so that I could get something to eat for me and my son and sometimes sell some of the vegetables which I planted. I would usually go and do the washing at Bongani's home since it was only his mother and father who were there. Old age was starting to catch up with his mother and she was ill with some disease she had been diagnosed with at the clinic, it did not allow her to do most of the chores around the house and I helped where I could. The pay was not much but it helped where needed. My husband started to become a stranger. All the promises were slowly broken. I would fall asleep crying and wake up with a swollen face. I could not go and cry to my mother. The whole village would have laughed at me for being a failure, the fact that I was a firstborn with 4 other siblings which were also females did not help. If ever I chose to separate from my husband, the whole village would have labelled me a failure and I could not put my parents through such humiliation.

Bongani would visit his home and he still had not chosen any of the girls in our village. When my son was 5 years old, I heard that it was his graduation party. I was also invited. Going there he had come with a girlfriend. Very different from the rest of us. She was everything we were not, and we started talking. We started exchanging whispers saying that Bongani thinks he is better than the rest of us. We started asking one another if we had seen the girl who is the girlfriend. Everyone wanted to see this girl who had just gotten famous.

By that time, my marriage had become history in the middle of a small village. Things had only worsened. I had become numb to all the pain my husband put me through. It did not matter anymore. I was now officially working at Bongani's home and it distracted me from thinking too much. Anyway, the graduation party was a success and Bongani's parents were happy that their son had made it. We went in numbers so that we could see the girl and exchange gossip amongst ourselves. She was beautiful, her name was Tumelo, she had gone to the same university as Bongani, but they were not doing the same course.

She was pale light, average height, and not too thick or thin either, she had a mole next to her left eyebrow. Her teeth were white, and she had a gap that was beautiful and made one want to see her smile every time. She was beautiful. To top it all, she had dimples and her eyes shone. We believed she was full of herself because she did not talk to anyone. She was nothing like our kind and open Bongani. She was totally different to him, to us, and that was because she thought she was better than the rest of us. Word had it that Bongani's father did not like the girl either because she was not from the same tribe as us and Bongani was supposed to marry a girl from our village, like all the other boys in the village. We trumped over that and we hoped that the son could listen to his father and choose the girl from his own people.

Months later, Bongani came back home and announced that he was going to marry the girl. His father was enraged. We were all disappointed at the young man's decision. All the girls who had hoped to be chosen by him were shocked on hearing the news. The young man had made his decision and there was nothing his father could do about it. He had saved enough for the wedding and so the wedding soon took place. In our village, we only did a traditional wedding, and that was what was expected from Bongani also. Tumelo could not do the traditional wedding because she was religious and Bongani wanted to make her happy. He allowed there to only be an English wedding. Bongani's parents were not impressed, especially his father. He was convinced that the girl had used a love potion on his son. All the traditional rituals which are done to welcome a new wife in the family were not done to Tumelo.

Her father-in-law told his son that, then it means she should never be fully a bride at his house since the rituals could not be done to her like other new brides. Bongani spoke to her about it and she was willing to compromise. She respected her husband and wanted to do right by him and his family. She was poured with a cow's bile to welcome her in the family as

Bongani's father had requested, at least that was the most important thing and now she could be regarded as the bride, 'umakoti', fully. We had felt that she compromised and allowed that to happen out of the respect she had for Bongani and his family, otherwise, the ritual meant nothing to her, we added amongst ourselves. She did not care about our culture and she did not belong to be one of us. We hated her for stealing our Bongani and failing to give him the respect that he deserves as a man. We could have done better. A normal person on his senses would not allow something like that, not in our village. Bongani organised everything and the wedding took place. It was a big white wedding and the whole village came to see for themselves what would happen. We would only see weddings like those in newspapers and only heard about them from other people. Everything was beautiful and both the bride and groom seemed happy. Hope was lost in the young girls from our village who were wishing that they still stood a chance with Bongani. Tumelo had marked her territory. We cursed under our breath and called the poor girl names.

The girl stayed for a few weeks before she finally went back to the Cities, something which was not normal in our village. The bride had to stay in her new family because it was believed that when you marry into a family, you do not only marry the man but the whole family. It was a different story with Tumelo, she was a qualified nurse, and Bongani had no problems with that. His father put pressure on him until it was agreed that Tumelo would relocate to stay with us. She was going to be a housewife like most of the women in our village. I did not stop working at their home even though Tumelo was now going to stay at home. Bongani's father understood that I needed the money and so I did what I could around the house, even with

Tumelo around. Bongani came almost every weekend. He never made a mistake. Tumelo fell pregnant that same year and Bongani decided that he was going to relocate and work from home so that he could take care of her. Relocating was not going to be a problem as he was now a Senior Civil Engineer and was now driving a car from the company for which he was working. We spoke saying that this girl fed our boy a love potion, as to how he did things was not normal in our village. We despised the girl even though he had done nothing to us. Perhaps this was because ours was a close community, so injury to one was an injury to all. Some of us had never even seen, nor spoken to her.

Tumelo was reserved and she enjoyed her time alone. At least I was lucky enough to get an insight into her disposition. I remember at first when she came to live at Bongani's, things were awkward between us until one evening we broke the ice and started to talk. She could speak and understand our language, but you could tell when she was talking that she is not as fluent in the language as all of us. One could tell that she had her own, and she was 'not one of us" as we all described her behind closed doors. I realised that she was actually a nice person. A contradiction to most of the things that people who usually went to clinics or hospitals usually said about nurses. Kind, smart and very humble. I liked her. By that time, my son had already started school, so I no longer came with him to work. While I was going to work, he would go to school. After Bongani had relocated he built a two-roomed house for him and his wife,

"Why didn't he build a house for his parents first? Why did he build a house for his girlfriend first?" we started whispering amongst ourselves. We did not even regard the fact that she was now his wife. What we did not know was that Bongani wanted to first build the house for him and his wife since he was relocating and then afterwards build a bigger one for his parents. We called the girl names again and cursed her under our breaths for stealing the son which we had raised so hard. Each one of us never had a good thing to say about "that girl". Yes, that is how we called her. We did not even know her name, nor did we bother.

Bongani and Tumelo were in love. I witnessed their love, lucky for me. They laughed and talked and joked around. Looking at them brought hope to me that perhaps love awaits us all. I remembered days of the in-love experience with my so-called husband who had become a stranger to me. The father of my child and my supposed husband became a stranger, just like that. I did not bother him or our families. I lived my life for myself and the beautiful blessing that God had trusted me with, my son. He kept me going. If it was not for him, I would have been depressed. The stories about him changing girls did not help, but I continued like a limping dog. Bongani's family became my other family. I was more than just the help, they treated me well, even Tumelo. Especially Tumelo. She was also in love, both her and her husband. It was uplifting to see people so much in love, even after all the time they had been together. Indeed, Bongani did build a big house for his parents towards the end of the year which followed. There were no whispers about this. We only congratulated his parents for having such a responsible son. Their beautiful daughter was a year and a few months old now. Bongani was crazy about his princess. They were a little happy family! We suspected that the child was not Bongani's. She resembled no one in the family. We loathed this girl for playing with our Bongani like that.

One morning, before going to work, Tumelo panickily knocked on my door. "Bongani is ill," she said. Her eyes were red. It did not seem like she had had any sleep the night before. Her face was covered in intense sadness. I quickly wore something appropriate and rushed with her to their house. She had already called an ambulance, so she said. And it was already on its way. Bongani was sweating, abnormally. It seemed he had shortness of breath and he seemed pale. Tumelo seemed she had lost weight in just one night. I went to the big house of Bongani's parents and told them about what was happening. They rushed to the room to check on their son. His mother was hysterical. When the ambulance arrived, Bongani's father refused that he be taken to hospital. He said that he was going to cook herbs and bring his son back to life.

We were already whispering. We knew what the cause of Bongani's illness was, even though nobody had told us. It was Tumelo. She bewitched him. That was for sure. We resented this girl from the Cities who was not even one of us. She had made our son ill. She was hoping to take him to 'hospital' so that she could easily finish him off. She was evil. She had made our son fall for her, took him to stay with her, she was still angry that she had to quit work and focus on her wifely duties and that is why she wanted to kill him. Selfish girl! That was the story. Nobody had told it to us, but it was true. Our poor Bongani.

When the ambulance arrived, Bongani's father fought with the paramedics who were trying to make the old man understand that his son needed medical attention. After a lot of arguing and tears, it was agreed by the paramedics that at least the son's wife should decide what was to happen with her husband. Tumelo decided that Bongani must be taken to hospital, but the father still refused. Bongani was brought back to the house, he could not walk anymore and needed our help. The old man started preparing his herbs. His wife helped. The paramedics had no choice but to leave and so they did. We sat with Bongani while waiting for his father to give him his herbs. Unfortunately, he could no longer wait. He sent us for water saying his throat is dry. He insisted that we both go and bring him also another blanket because he was feeling cold. Coming back, he was lifeless. I went to fetch the water, his wife the blanket. I rushed back when I heard Tumelo's screams from the kitchen. Bongani had died. His father went to lock himself in his bedroom and said nothing to no one. The women I was sitting with were broken. The dead man's wife was broken.

She killed him, we said. She killed the man who loved her, who had made her a wife and impregnated her. The man whom she loved, but we did not know that, neither did we care. We had drawn our conclusions and we were not willing to listen to any version which did not match ours. We called the wife names. Our accusations were unsubstantiated, and our stories had no lucidity. We did not care how she felt. She had killed our son. Bongani was buried in the weekend that followed. His mother was a walking zombie. His father became a shadow of the man he was before he allowed his son to marry a woman who was going to kill him in the end. He blamed himself, and this girl who was toxic. If only he had put his foot down early about his son going to the hospital. Maybe he would have been able to save his son's life. He was angry at Tumelo. The deceased's wife was shattered. The bereaved family was hurt. The community was talking. The widow's family did come to support her, but it was just only her elder sister and her friend. Apparently, they were orphans. The only family Tumelo had was her sister and Bongani's family. I tried to force her to eat with no success. Everybody was blaming her for the death of her husband, and yet nobody asked her how she felt.

Two days after the funeral, when everyone had gone back to their homes, I went to her room to give her food. She was hanging there, lifeless. I never understood if she at least had thought about the fact that she was pregnant with their secondborn. She had confided in me one morning. She was a few weeks but she was happy to be expecting with her husband. I do not even think she had thought about their elder daughter. It did not matter anymore though because she was dead, with the baby in her womb.

3 – DEAR DIARY

She has been avoiding her Diary, of late. She tells it things that she tells no one and shares with it her deepest secrets, her thoughts and how she truly feels about things. The Diary is like a best friend to her which she unloads onto. She always carries it with her and she never loses sight of it. Nobody has ever read it, except for him. She has never even allowed her only friend, Thembelihle to read it. She has been avoiding it lately because she knows she has bad news for it. She does not want to face the reality of what she is supposed to share with it. She looks at it as it rests on her study table and she blinks more than she used to just a few moments ago. It all comes back to ambush her. She feels and thinks about it all. Everything returns in full force. She quickly takes it and decides to write it all as raw as it is in both her mind and heart...

"Dear Diary.

You are my true and best friend of them all. You know me the same way as you know yourself, if not more. You have witnessed how hard it was for me for the past two months and a few days. I have been a mess Diary. I am failing, Diary, I really am. I cannot live without Mpho. He is all that I think about. I love him, and I will live to regret the day we laid eyes on each other for the first time. I hate myself for loving him so much. I would do anything to stop. I think loving someone like this is not healthy. How do you love someone who has proven every chance he got that he resents you? Worse, he is destroying me and has no idea about it. He hurt me, Diary! He hurt me so much, but he is still the first person I think about in the morning and the last at night. Why do I love him so much? I want to stop Diary. I need to stop!"

She is crying and can no longer continue. It all comes back…

Mpho and Nozi met four years before when Nozi was doing her grade ten. They had a school trip from their school to the nearest town. Nozi had always been friends with Lihle, and she spent more time with her then, as she did now. People never really paid much attention to her. Lihle always dominated and outshone her. Almost every time a guy would approach them, he'd be interested in Lihle. She had accepted it and had no problems with that. She was one of those girls whose presence is not felt, but when absent, they would be missed. She was beautiful, but one would not witness that beauty if one compared her with her friend. Unlike Lihle, Nozi was not a talker. Socializing was not her strong point either. On that school trip, four years back she met the guy whom she believed was the love of her life. Theirs was love at first sight, like in the movies and books. They were at the beach and their teachers were sitting at a distance not paying much attention to them. He came towards them and their eyes locked. For a moment there, time stood still. He was wearing only boxers and nothing else. He had sand on his hairy legs and his six-pack was exposed to the sun rays. Nozi was sure that she had seen this light-skinned and slim handsome guy somewhere, but she was not sure where. He had thick eyebrows and pink lips. He was hairy. Though a stranger, he looked familiar. She was just simply wearing her school uniform, a maroon printed skirt, a white short-sleeved shirt with a maroon pullover. Both her and Lihle were barefooted. They had left their bags with the rest of the other learners and had taken off their shoes so they could take a walk along the sea and enjoy its breeze. Nozi nearly died that day, she was in love, and up to today, she remembered it like it was yesterday.

When Mpho looked at Nozi that day, he found comfort in her dark black eyes which carefully stared at him with love. He had just broken up with his girlfriend. She chose another guy over him, and they were planning their wedding then. Mpho had not fully healed when he met Nozi, and he was not prepared to get into another relationship just yet. Meeting Nozi made him believe that his broken heart was going to heal more quickly and he could finally forget about his ex-girlfriend who was getting married in just a few weeks with another man. Mpho had finished his grade 12 the year before but could not go to tertiary or did not want to. His marks were good, but he did not bother applying. He was neither working nor studying, so his father took care of him like he always did. He spent his time visiting his paternal family and he enjoyed it. He had never met his mother. Apparently, she fought with his father when he was only five months and she left him with his paternal family. He only knew that side of his family and had taught himself to stop asking questions since nobody wanted to give him any answers. He had just wanted to relax and swim a little that day, to unwind a bit. He was tired of staying indoors and feeling sorry for himself.

"Hello ladies," he said to Lihle and Nozi, looking at Nozi. For the first time, a guy had greeted them interested in Nozi and not Lihle. Mpho requested to speak to Nozi, and Lihle excused herself. They clicked. Their conversation flowed, and they exchanged numbers. They talked until Lihle came to call Nozi when it was time to go and their teachers were losing patience. If it were up to them both, they'd have spent the rest of the day, perhaps the rest of their lives, together. They said their goodbyes and parted ways, promising that they'd communicate with each other. They kept their promise and kept the communication going. A few days later they were an item. Nozi had only had a boyfriend when she was doing grade 8. Things never got serious and he left her when he changed schools. They were forced to cut ties because his whole family was moving to another province. Nozi was hurt, but she soon got over the hurt because they had been together for only a month. Since then, she had never fallen in love with anyone else.

When Mpho told her about his ex-girlfriend Berlinda, who left him for a man who was working and had money, Nozi could see the hurt in his eyes. That was three years back when Nozi was doing grade 11. Their relationship was stable and Nozi saw her whole future in Mpho. She was planning her life around him. She wanted to spend her whole life with him. Berlinda had broken him, but Nozi came to heal his broken heart. Mpho had loved Berlinda with his whole heart, regardless of all the negative things his friends had been saying about her. She was 3 years older than him, but that did not stop his heart from choosing and loving her. It was only a pity that in the end, she broke his heart. He had fully healed and was grateful to Nozi for coming to his life when she did when he needed her most. He had gotten over the hurt Berlinda had caused him.

They had been through quite a lot together. Nozi had never once given up on Mpho, even when he'd made a laughingstock out of her. He would cheat on her with many girls from her school, who were older than her. Mpho would visit his uncle who drove taxis and lived next to Nozi's school so it could be easy for him to see her, and his other girlfriends. Nozi remembers the first day he told him of his uncle. The first day they spoke at the beach, she had realized that she knew him from somewhere. Maybe theirs was not love at first sight, after all. Nozi would be heartbroken but would go back to him in the end. She always chose him. When Nozi was doing her grade 11, a year after she had met Mpho, she was still a virgin. Mpho would cheat on her and blame her for refusing to sleep with him. That same year when they were approaching their final exams, Nozi found out that Mpho had impregnated her classmate. She was so heartbroken and was not able to study. She was so hurt having to see the girl every day, and the growing stomach was evidence that her boyfriend had betrayed her. She started bunking classes and could not handle all the pressure which came with the heartbreak. She was so broken and did not make it. She failed and had to repeat her grade 11. Her mother had promised to buy her a laptop so that it would be easy to study in matric. She just wanted to encourage her. She was so disappointed when she heard that her daughter had failed. Nozi's friend, Lihle told her to break up with Mpho before he destroyed her, but Nozi forgave him and they moved in together. Mpho promised that he was never going to break her heart again, and a part of her believed him. She gave him another chance. Who could blame her? Her love for him was just too much.

When she was doing her grade 11 for the second time, Mpho proved to her to be a changed man. He was faithful and did not cheat on her. He was supportive of her and he was a good father to his son. He supported him financially and would visit if ever he got a chance. He was no longer dating his mother, but they were trying to be great parents to their son. Nozi was there and she encouraged him to be present in his son's life in every way. He was now working at a Store doing general work and sometimes being a cashier. The money was not much, but on weekends he'd DJ in parties or functions. That is how he made some extra cash. Mpho's father stopped giving him his monthly allowance the day he heard that he had impregnated a girl. He started sending the money to the girl and his grandson once he was born. Life was okay, simple. Nozi and Mpho were happy and their relationship was stable.

Results came and Nozi had passed. She was so happy and Mpho too was happy for her. Unfortunately, that year her mother could not buy her the laptop. She had financial problems, and her daughter understood. Hers was a job that did not pay much. She worked at a bank and led a normal life. Nozi was her only child and they lived alone, just the two of them. Nozi's father had his other family. Although he was not married, he did what other people would call cohabiting with his children's mother and their 4 children. Rumour had it that he also had another 3 children from different mothers, besides Nozi, with who he had no relationship. He sometimes called to check on her, but their relationship was not healthy. He would send money sometimes, or if Nozi called and requested it. She never visited him, and he never requested her to. Nozi had planned to remain a virgin until marriage. She wanted to make her mother proud and make up for all the trouble she had caused her. Her mother had promised her a massive 21st birthday party, that was if she could reach 21 years still a virgin. Mpho could not wait anymore. He had waited for the whole year and a half, he would say. He was a guy, he said, and could no longer wait for Nozi. He broke up with her and said he wanted freedom and to sleep with whomever he wanted to sleep with, without breaking her heart. Since she was not ready, he wanted someone else who'd trust him and be able to "meet his needs as a guy". Again, Nozi was hurt. She just could not lose Mpho, she loved him too much. She trusted Mpho and she believed that he would never hurt her. She begged him not to leave her. That same week, Mpho took her virginity. They were happy and Mpho promised that he was going to make her his wife. She was his ideal girlfriend, he would say. She had no regrets choosing him, Nozi would think. He was the one for her.

Late the year before, when Nozi was doing her grade 12, a girl called her anonymously and told her to break up with Mpho because he was her man. She swore at her and called her names. Nozi just laughed at the girl. She had no reason to be angry, she had thought. The girl was probably one of the many girls who had a crush on her man. She did not even bother to tell or ask Mpho about her. Their love and relationship were strong, and she did not want to focus on things that could sabotage it. A week passed, and the same girl called her. She begged her to leave her man alone. That was when she decided to take Mpho's cellphone and played detective. She found pictures of her, she assumed. She also found text messages between Mpho and her. It seemed like their love was still new and they were happy. Nozi felt her heart breaking that very moment. After everything, Mpho was still cheating, with another woman, not with his son's mother. Nozi was in the middle of her trial exams when this happened. She tried to be strong. She did not want to repeat the same mistake she did, which led to her failing and repeating her grade 11. She just could not disappoint her mother again. She did not confront

Mpho about it and she let herself be consumed by the pain. She let everything be motivation to her. She studied hard until she was done with her final exams. It was hard though because she'd sometimes not eat and not be able to study. She started to lose weight. Her life was a mess. Her marks did not allow her to study Clinical Psychology, so she ended up upgrading, as she was now. Mpho was distant all the time. He started slowly drifting away.

Two months before, the same girl posted pictures of her and Mpho on Facebook and tagged him. Nozi had not been feeling well for days and she did not know what was wrong with her. She naturally hated clinics and hospitals, so she did not go to see a doctor. She just thought it would pass soon. Then this other day while she had just woken up from her daily nap, she was naturally a sleeper, at her room and had just finished preparing something to eat, she logged into Facebook. She was reading through newsfeeds when she saw pictures of Mpho and the other girl. They looked so happy, and Mpho had commented on the pictures that he was going to make the girl his wife, something which he had said to her the previous year after he had taken her virginity. The girl had replied and declared her own love for Mpho. The glass of water which she was holding fell and cracked. Nozi felt a sharp and very painful pain in her abdomen. The pain was warm, and it was soon followed by unbearable stomach cramps. She felt a headache and before she knew it, she had fallen. Luckily, her mother had just come back from work and when she did not reply when she shouted her name, she went to check her in her room, to find her on the floor unconscious. Her mother took her to hospital immediately and was attended to by a doctor. She was pregnant and had a miscarriage. Nozi was shattered. Both by the fact that her man cheated on her and mostly broken because she had lost her baby. When Mpho came she decided to confront him about the other girl and he plainly denied it. That, alone, broke her heart. She had all proof that Mpho was cheating but he did want to admit it. That just broke her heart into pieces.

Finally, Mpho admitted to his mistakes and apologized. He seemed genuine and Nozi decided to forgive him. She had forgiven him but had made it clear to him that she was not going to be in a relationship with him anymore. She had to protect her heart, and she could not do that while he was still a part of her life. She had thought that her life should be much easier with him out of it, but it seemed to be the opposite of that. He was the only thing her mind deemed important, for it never got tired of thinking of him. She had found herself having had dialled his cellphone number countless times and would defeat the cravings of hearing at least his voice. Many guys had asked her out, but she was not ready to be in a relationship with someone else. She was hoping that maybe one day, hers was a happily ever after on its way, with Mpho. She was hoping for a different reality, where she could be pregnant again and give birth to a beautiful baby boy, one to which Mpho would be a responsible father. She wanted a reality where she and Mpho could get married and have lots and lots of fun together.

She has been staring at her Diary which continues lying peacefully on the table. She looks at her cellphone which is charging next to the Diary and her hopeless love gets the better of her. It defeats her. She quickly takes the cellphone, as though to make sure that she makes that call soon enough before she changes her mind, or her heart. It rings for quite some time before a girl's soft voice answers, "Hello?" Nozi does not know what to make of this. This is something she had not expected.

She quickly drops the call, almost as quickly as she had made it. Her mouth gets dry and she suddenly feels just tired. Her cellphone rings. Checking the I. D., she realizes that it is the same person she had called a few seconds ago. She answers hesitantly, "H-Hello."

"Nozi," he says. A pause. It feels like it has been at least five years since she last heard his voice.

"Mpho," she finally says. An unexpected cold shiver settles on his stomach. He could never be ready to hear her voice, he realizes. "Why, Mpho? Why did you break my heart so much?"

Not only was he not ready to hear her voice, but he was also not ready for this kind of question, he thinks to himself. He tries to gather his thoughts, but he just does not know what to say. He keeps quiet. She realizes that she has dropped the call and her breathing has changed. Her chest is burning. It feels like there is a burning fire inside her. The pain comes all over again to consume her. She takes the pen she had unintentionally put down and continues to write her Diary.

"I have made the biggest fool out of myself, Diary. For months I have been crying myself to sleep, struggling to keep up with my schoolwork, I have been so broken. Guess what? The person who is the reason behind all that is living his life to the fullest, with no care in the world. I have been a ghost of the girl I was before I met my worst nightmare. Meanwhile, he has been living his best life. I have been miserable, and yet he could not wait to move on with his life without me. I am an idiot, Dear Diary. A pure idiot!" Tears are wetting the poor Diary, which not only has to be the bearer of all this bad news but also of all the tears which wet it. Her cellphone rings again.

"Please just do not drop, Nozi. I am so sorry."

Those words cut deep down in the pieces she believes that her heart has become. They awoke all the emotions she had been trying to lull to sleep these past two months. "What are you sorry for Mpho? What exactly is it that you are sorry for? Are you sorry for approaching and proposing to me four years ago when I was in grade ten, or for that I loved you hugely, truly and honestly? Are you sorry that I trusted you with my life, or that you broke that trust by constantly cheating on me with different girls because I would not sleep with you? What are you sorry for? For taking my virginity. For impregnating my classmate in grade eleven. For still cheating on me even after I had given you my virginity. Remember I failed my grade 11 and disappointed my mother. Is that what you are sorry for? Are you sorry for making me pregnant or for causing my miscarriage? The past two months have been hell. I had never felt so much pain in my life. Are you sorry for that? Are you sorry for the fact that while I was breaking apart because of you, you were moving on with your life just fine? What is it that you are sorry for, Mpho?" She is screaming and shouting at him now. This was not part of the plan. Her emotions always get the better of her. Nobody says anything.

Mpho decides to leave the room and go outside. He could not talk with Nozi with his fiancée eavesdropping. Yes, he had proposed to the girl Nozi saw on his profile on Facebook two months back. They had not decided on the date of their wedding, nor had they started with its preparations, but they were both happy. "Do you think you could forgive me, Nozi? Ever in your life?" he finally asks.

"But why did you hurt me so much Mpho? Why? I had never done anything wrong to you."

He honestly does not know what to say.

"When are you getting married to her? You said you were going to make her your wife." She did not know that as they spoke, Mpho was engaged to the girl.

"Please Nozi, do not do that. That is not important."

"I wish the both of you the best of luck, and no, that does not come from a bad place. You are a good guy, Mpho. Of course, you are not perfect, but you are a good guy and a great father to your son. I know you would also have made a good father to our baby." A pause. She swallows. "Please treat her well, Mpho. Not like you treated me. Respect her for a change. I shall always love you and I forgive you, whatever it is that you are sorry for."

She drops the call without saying goodbye. She is truly and deeply hurt. She decides to go and take a long and well-deserved shower. She is still crying. She leaves the Diary open like that with stains of her still wet tears. She arrives at the bathroom and opens the water to flow and meet her nakedness. She falls and lets the water flow on her. She sobs. She is hurt. She takes a razor and begins to cut. She cut first her thighs. She has been so empty and wants to assure her that she is still alive. Can still feel. However, she does not want to feel the emotional pain. She wants to escape it. The physical pain is bearable, she thinks. She cuts her wrists. She bleeds. She meets the beginning of her unknown ending.

4 – MEMORIES AND MORE OF THEM

As I browse through my cellphone, I find myself staring at his picture. In my mind a picture of the small coffin, everything rushes to my mind, all at once. I could never argue with anyone about life's unfairness. I have been at the receiving end for much too long.

I still remember the day my parents got married. I was 17 years, doing grade 11. My father had finally saved enough to give my mother the wedding of her dreams. He often promised her that he was going to give it to her. I could no longer be a flower girl as I had always imagined myself growing up, instead, I was one of the bridesmaids. People always said my mother and I seem more like sisters than mother and daughter. Around that time, I had already gotten used to that. She also. My aunt, her sister, would usually say, perhaps it was because she got pregnant with me when she was just a teenager, 16 years old. My too-big body for my age did not help. I was "chubby", as my classmates would sometimes say. Growing up, I used to have really low self-esteem because other learners at school would call me funny names because of my "big body". I do not think one ever gets over all the insults and all, we just grow up and teach ourselves to forget. My parents always made sure that I felt as beautiful as possible. I do not think I could have gotten through it all without them. I have lost weight throughout the years, though, but that is a story for another day. My brother, Banele, was 4 years old and they made him a page boy with my aunt's daughter who was a flower girl.

I had never seen my mother that beautiful, nor as happy. She was finally getting married to the love of her life, my very own father. Like any couple, they fought and went through things, but through my parents, I learnt what true love is. I have always described myself as "lucky" whenever I think of my parents and the love they shared, for I witnessed it, first hand, something a lot of children nowadays do not experience from their parents because of reasons I would rather not get into.

My mother was a housewife, although she did achieve a diploma in administration, and my father, a male nurse. My father was my role model. I wanted to follow in his footsteps when I finished school. I also wanted to be a nurse and do music in my spare time, something I loved passionately. My father did not allow my mother to go to work. He said that he was going to take care of her, and he did. For a long time, I stayed being the only child and they showered me with love. They made sure I always felt like their little princess, and that is one thing I will always be grateful for to them, the love. My mother cleaned the house, cooked and took care of our home, while my father went to work. I do not remember even a single day coming back from school and not having anything to eat. Sometimes on weekends or if my father was off at work, he would help my mother around the house, I also. When I was a child, I could not understand why it was so necessary that they hug each other every morning. Sometimes, my father would get out of the car and go back inside the house as though he had forgotten something, just so he could hug my mother.

Back when I was in primary school, my father gave me a lift every morning and dropped me off at school because the way to his workplace, the clinic at which he worked, passed there. When he was off, I would take a walk to school and that never bothered me. I only started walking every day when I was in high school because the school was not far. I know you must probably be thinking that my parents were living in sin, and that is not correct. Though both my parents were educated, they were also very cultural, especially my father. He had paid for everything that was due to my grandparents. The lobola negotiations had taken place and they had married at Home Affairs. The only thing that left was the big wedding which my mother always spoke about. I seldom saw my parents fight. Seldom. Even if they did, but they would sleep laughing again, and things would go back to normal. One thing which always confused me was that, even though they would fight, but my father never left home not having hugged my mother. My mother also never resisted. I think it had become natural, something which he could not start his day without doing. The white big wedding was just a formality, and of course, a promise my father had to keep, but my parents were so in love.

The wedding was attended by a lot of people from different places. There were a lot of cars. The venue had been decorated so beautifully. I wore makeup for the first time. I was happy that my mother's dream had finally turned into a reality. I remember when she walked down the aisle, held tightly by one of her uncles to give her to my father, she was quietly sobbing. My father stood like a gentleman that he was and patiently waited to take her hand. As they faced the pastor, I remember him gentle wiping her tears with the palm of his left hand. He gave her an assuring look as if to say, "I shall always be here. It's finally happening. Relax!" My mother pulled herself together and by the time they said their vows, she seemed a lot whole better. I remember my aunt closing my eyes with her hand when the pastor said, "You may kiss the bride." She had always been a drama queen. She was the maid of honour. I laughed looking at her, pretending to close my eyes. I have always loved singing. My aunt and I had planned that I was going to write a song and sing it for my parents. I could see they were surprised when the program director called my name and said I had something to share with everyone. Being a victim of body shaming at school had had its toll on me. Even though I knew I was a good singer and I loved singing but standing in front of a crowd was not very easy. The only thing which kept me going then was knowing how what I was about to do was going to make my parents happy. Besides, doing something you love is life. It's like you forget that there is anyone else in the world other than you. Singing took me to places that I know for a fact that I could never go to, physically. The smile on my parent's faces as the audience applauded was priceless. They were truly happy. If the hands of time could be turned back, I would always go back to that day, or not.

It was planned that my parents were going to leave for their honeymoon that same day. I kind of envied them. I could have used some time out, alone though, especially since I had just finished writing my final exams. I did not have any friends or a boyfriend. I could say that my friends were my parents and my younger brother. I did not see any need for a boyfriend. I was okay alone. Have you ever felt like going far away alone, just to regroup and get some fresh air? That is exactly how I felt. Being called names at school had made me distant. Sometimes I would feel like being alone for no reason at all. I was happy for my parents though, I could tell they were going to have a good time, and they deserved it. They had already packed, and they were just going to take all their luggage and leave. We were then going to stay behind and make sure that everything was in order, with my aunt and grandmother and my mother's two uncles. My parents needed their break. My father had saved enough for the honeymoon also and everything had been organized already. He did not earn much, considering the bills he had to pay every month, but he had planned everything for years. It also helped that my mother was a simple woman who did not like too much fancy stuff. They were going to spend two weeks on their honeymoon. That whole time, Banele and I were going to visit granny and aunt. Her daughter, Amkela, our cousin stayed with her paternal family. My parents left in the late afternoon.

It had been a long day. Everyone was tired and my parents had left for their honeymoon. We had planned that we were going to start sorting everything the following day with an aunt. We were all getting ready to sleep just after seven when aunt's cellphone rang. She tiredly answered and spoke for some time with the person on the other line. She suddenly dropped the cell phone and tears started flowing on her cheeks. Granny was so frightened she put my brother down on one of the couches as he was sitting on her lap and rushed to my aunt. Banele had already fallen asleep on her lap. Granny loved us with Banele. She always visited our home and when school closed, we would also visit her. We loved her also.

"What is happening?" she quickly asked.

"There was an accident, Ma," aunt replied softly.

"How are they?" I asked as I got close to the two women whose faces were filled with confusion and despair.

"That was one of the paramedics. They arrived at the scene too late. They were too injured and had already lost too much blood. Neither of them made it."

Years after, those words still haunt me up to this day. I still hear aunty saying them. Without a word, granny went down on her knees and prayed. She prayed and tears were flowing uncontrollably from her eyes. I could never get a picture of her helpless kneeling and praying in my mind. Granny is one of those women who are usually described as 'strong'. Growing up I heard that she used to have 9 children, but she had lost 5 to death and was now only left with four. She is the woman who saw her children perish in front of her and she had to bury them. That was not all, she had to bury the love of her life also, who fell sick and lost the battle when I was doing grade 9, two years before.

So, granny carried all that burden with pride of being a 'strong' woman and a prayer warrior. Banele started to be restless, as though he was having a nightmare. He woke up and cried. Aunt quickly went to calm him down, trying her best in vain to hide her own tears which wanted her to know the meaning of betrayal. They sat on the couch with Banele on her lap while brushing his head and trying to wipe his tears with her other hand. Granny did not stop praying. People always describe heartbreak and what it means to be hurt. If I had to describe how I felt at that very moment, anything I would say would not be true. I could never describe the feelings which rushed to ensnare my heart at that very moment.

What I know, however, is that I had never felt so much pain before. I stood there, letting all the feelings sink in, letting the reality that I was now an orphan find its seat and settle down in my heart. On their wedding day, my parents lost their lives.

The day which was supposed to be their happiest became their last in the world, and the most painful for their loved ones, myself included.

"Thandiwe. Hurry, go and fetch your brother's inhaler!" My brother was having an asthma attack. I would have given anything just to not see my brother like that. He naturally was asthmatic. As an infant, Banele frequently got ill. He would have laboured breathing and would wheeze. My parents took him to a doctor, and he was diagnosed with asthma. He had inherited the disease from my mother. I often heard my mother talking about an asthma action plan which she had with the doctor. And Banele was given an inhaler to soothe him if ever he had an asthma attack. I quickly searched Banele's back bag and took his inhaler and gave it to Aunt. We never made the mistake of leaving his inhaler at home, whenever he went somewhere. Aunt quickly helped him sit up straight. She then made him take one puff of a rescue inhaler. Banele rarely had asthma attacks. My mother always tried reducing exposure for him to all his triggers. He then got better in a few minutes. Granny took him and she lulled him to sleep. She had finished praying. He slept with her that night, and I slept with Aunt. Other nights when we visited, we both shared a bed with Granny and Aunt slept alone in her room or with Amkela if she had visited. I could not bear seeing my grandmother like that. I slept with Aunt because she was trying to contain herself. I needed to sleep and forget, even if it was going to be just for a few hours.

While in bed, I could feel that Aunt was not sleeping. Her thoughts were probably ganging up on her like mine were doing. She was restless. There were no small talks like there usually were whenever we were together, that night. I wanted to cry and let everything out, but something inside me did not believe what was happening. I was sure that maybe the paramedics were mistaken. I knew they were going to call and apologize in the morning for the mistake they had made of wishing death upon my parents. My parents were still alive, and as we slept, they were enjoying their honeymoon. I remember calling both their cellphones with no success.

My father's cellphone went straight to voicemail and my mother's kept ringing and no one was answering. I do not remember when I fell asleep, but when I woke up the next day, Aunt was not in bed. I went straight to Granny's room. There was only Banele there who was fast asleep. I did not want to interrupt him, so I went on to the dining room. Granny was with many of the neighbours. I quickly went back to Granny's room before any of them could see me. I went to sleep with my brother. We held each other tight until I fell asleep again. Life had a sour taste. Later that day, we went back home with Banele, Aunt, and Granny. The walls were hostile like they were impatiently waiting for the arrival of someone, or two. The funeral arrangements proceeded.

The funeral took place on the weekend which followed. The irony. Two consecutive weekends, one on which they got married, followed by their funeral. I do not remember much of that day. Anyone who has lost a loved one would attest to me. The finality which comes with the moment when one is called to pour soil on the grave could never be compared to anything. That moment is like an awakening that roughly invites you back to reality. The tears no longer come. Everything remains numb and you just do it. My parents were buried that day. I was never the same after that day. I shall never be the same.

A week before schools opened, I heard that there was a competition for singing in our community hall. Aunt encouraged me to go and told me how much faith she had in me. I decided to enter the competition even though I was not very keen. The competition was very tough. Everyone had come prepared, and they all knew their story. I had also prepared, and Aunt was my biggest fan. Every time while practising, my grandmother would stay with Banele and Aunt would be my judge and facilitate my singing. The day came and I got second.

This guy, Mthobisi had come to visit for the holidays. One would not say he was handsome. He was also not ugly. Just the average. But his voice! Before the judges even announced who had won, the audience already knew it was him. I did not mind him, but I have always been a good loser, life had long taught me to have no problem with losing. Aunt tried to console me until she realized I was really okay. Aunt had to go somewhere so she left me behind. Mthobisi came to congratulate me or to boast. I really did not have any energy to waste on him, so I just looked at him and he talked and talked. One thing I realized about him was that he loved himself too much, abnormally, especially for a guy and he would talk about himself until Jesus comes back. He praised himself and spoke about all the awards his voice had won him in the past. As if I cared. I just let him be. I went back home and late that night I got a call from a number I did not know.

I would have never guessed. It was Mthobisi. Apparently, he was interested in me and would love to get to know me better. He did not say where he had gotten my number and I did not ask anything either. It was my first time getting attention from a guy outside of my family. He was even better than earlier and spoke like a normal human being. We agreed to meet the following day. I was worried. I did not know how to react and there was no one I could talk and share my feelings with. I was quite nervous. We met and he was still the same humbled gentleman whom I had spoken with the evening before over the call.

There were moments though where he would talk nonstop about himself, but he would then give me a chance to talk also. It did not seem like he saw anything wrong when he did his thing of talking nonstop about himself. The meetings continued and meeting up with him became the norm almost every day before schools opened. To cut a long story short, we got into a relationship two days before schools opened. He had to leave that same day but decided to stay for obvious reasons. He was a Pharmacy student at Rhodes University in the Eastern Cape Province.

He told me they were only going to be required to go back on Campus two weeks after and so he decided to spend the remaining time with me. I felt special. I did not tell anyone about the relationship. My grandmother and aunt realized that I had changed and asked me what was wrong, but I did not reply and give them any tangible answer, so they let it all go. I was crazy, literally, about Mthobisi. He was the first person to show any care towards my feelings and thoughts after my parents. He was my pillar and always knew what to say. He was the first person to whom I spoke about my parents and how truly broken I was to lose both on the same day and having to attend their funeral on the weekend which followed their wedding. I told him how difficult it was when I had to let the reality that I was now an orphan sink in and how I wanted to hold on to that soil at their funeral when we were called to pour soil in their grave but decided to just let it go instead. I wanted to not let go of the only friends God had given me but decided to take them so soon. I told him of the nights I would stay awake asking God what Banele and I had done so wrong that He had decided to take our parents from us so soon, getting no answer. He was there and gave me a shoulder to cry on.

The holidays ended for Mthobisi and things changed. I was in grade 12, in love, parentless and homesick for someone whom I could not be with. Mthobisi went back to school and left me. Things were not the same. He never called or tried to communicate. I would try to contact him, but he had no time for me. I let him be and focused on my studies and my family, especially Banele because it felt like I had a responsibility as his only elder sibling to take care of him. Mthobisi came back during the Easter holidays.

He apologized for being scarce and blamed it on his studies. He seemed sincere and so I forgave him. Things went back to normal. He helped me to apply for tertiary and I thanked God for having someone like him in my life. I was happy, for the first time since my parents died. I really enjoyed spending time with him even though it was only for a week. It did not help that we, the matriculants, only closed for 3 days, literally. Mthobisi would fetch me from school, and we'd walk and catch up. I enjoyed every minute I spent with him. He went promising to change for the better. Indeed, he did. He tried to text at least once a day if he could not call. I did not mind that because I also had to focus on my studies. Aunt got engaged to Amkela's father a few weeks from there. She was so happy, and so was Granny.

At the beginning of June, on a weekend of my Aunt's birthday, she got married to her fiancé. It was a happy day throughout. For me especially because Mthobisi had come back for the holidays. Aunt left to live with her in-laws permanently. I could see she was happy. I was happy for her.

I continued meeting up with Mthobisi whenever I could. I felt that I was ready to take things to the next level in our relationship. As much as Mthobisi tried to be patient and put no pressure on me, but I could see he was starting to get irritated. I gave my innocence and purity to him on those holidays, on one cold night after I had lied to Granny about a study group I had to attend with some classmates at a friend's home. I had never given her any reason not to trust me, so she believed my lie. As usual, he went back. We were both happily in love. There was nothing I could complain about. We used to talk every day when I was not busy with my studies. In the following holidays, he made sure to visit. And during the December holidays too. I was done with my exams and was just awaiting my results. I had given it my all, it was now up to the markers. Mthobisi never had any doubts that I was going to make it. I loved him so much.

In late December I started feeling ill. Mthobisi accompanied me to the clinic just a day before New Year's Eve. The nurse there took a pregnancy test and found out that I was 3 weeks pregnant. I was so scared. The thought that a small body, or fetus, or whatever it was called, at that stage, was living and growing inside of me really scared me. My grandmother was going to be so disappointed. We spoke with Mthobisi afterwards and decided that an abortion was the best option. He promised that he was going to support me every step of the way. We decided that it was best that I did not do it at the clinic, which is near home, the one my father used to work at. We went to the one which I was sure that no one knew who I was, and nobody bothered. I thought about the disappointment my parents were probably feeling looking down at me. I was surely a disgrace to them. We agreed that I was going to do it the day before the results came out. From there onwards I wanted to focus only on the positive things in my life.

The day came. Early that morning Granny got a call that there was an emergency at Auntie's home, so she had to leave to go there. I was then forced to cancel and stay with Banele. That was something I would not be able to do because I had decided that I was going to do what I had to do. My decision was final. I left Banele and promised him that I was going to come just after a few hours. We went with Mthobisi to the clinic. He had kept his word and accompanied me. The nurse who helped me took me for counselling first and wanted to know that I was sure before she could proceed with the process. I was certain. I was given pills and instructed to take one at that time and another before I slept that night. I went back home and Mthobisi suddenly gave me a silent treatment on our way back. I did not know what to do or say to him because I was also dealing with my own demons. And besides, the reason why he accompanied me was so that he could support me and not give me more headaches. I tried to talk to him, but he just kept quiet. For quite some time until I remembered that I had to leave since I had left Banele alone. I went back home and left the grumpy Mthobisi alone.

When I arrived home, I went to put the pill in my room before Granny came back and saw it. I then went to check up on Banele. When I checked he was fast asleep, or so I thought. It seemed like Banele had encountered a trigger for his Asthma. I was not there to help my brother and he finally lost his young life. His face seemed pale but at peace. I was so broken. When Granny came back, all was history. She was perplexed. If only I had not gone to the clinic, my brother would not have died. I had killed him. If only I came back early from the clinic, maybe that would not have happened. My heart broke. Granny called Aunt and uncles and other family members from my paternal family. Everybody was a mess. I just went to my room and cried. I wanted to be no part of anything. At midnight I started feeling my abdomen as though it was shaking. Switching the lights on I realized that I was bleeding. I was expecting it but the pain was unbearable. I slept in a fetus position and let the pains play their part. I closed my eyes trying to suppress the pain. And the realization landed on my mind. I had killed an innocent soul. Two innocent souls. I was a murderer. Tears found their way down my cheeks. I pushed the poor soul out of my body.

I woke up the next morning and was feeling so weak. I quickly woke up, bathed and washed the bedding before granny woke up. I went back to sleep and put on another bedding. I had switched my cellphone off the night before. Switching it on I found missed calls and congratulatory messages from my classmates. I had passed with a Bachelor, 4 B's and C's only. My grandmother was happy that I had made it. Even though Banele's death had taken its toll on her, but she really tried to be happy for me. She was so happy and proud of me. I was happy to know that I had made her proud. When she was done congratulating me she went to tell whoever was willing to listen that her granddaughter had passed. I had no missed call or message from Mthobisi. When I got on WhatsApp, I realized that he had blocked me. I tried to call but he had also blocked my number. I never bothered him or myself again. I believe he had his reasons for what he did, and I chose to respect them not even knowing what they were. Life had taught me to be a good loser so if he also was going to be one of my losses, then I could not and did not want to fight fate. I had lost a great deal and he was just a teardrop in an ocean. I believe life has to move on, whether or not one found closure.

My brother's funeral was on the week which followed. Everything was just a mess. As I saw the coffin slowly going down, I knew nothing could ever be the same again. I felt my soul leaving my body to rush and catch his body which lay peacefully in that small coffin. I could not shake the thought and feeling that I caused my brother's death. In just one day I had managed to take two lives, perhaps it's time I took mine.

"Sister Thandiwe, the Matron is requesting that you come to her office."

Without turning to look who that is, I just know that it is Akhona, our hospital receptionist. I quickly wipe my eyes, scroll down in my cellphone from the picture which it was displaying and go to the Matron's office. I really hope it is good news.

5 – FLAMES OF THE BARE BROWN PASTURES

Bonani had been having nightmares for the two previous nights. He didn't want to talk about it the first night when his wife asked what was wrong, the second night she didn't bother asking because she could see that her husband did not want to talk about whatever was troubling him. It was the third night and Bonani was crying loudly and speaking something Mandulo could not understand. She then decided to go and clear her mind, on the big rock near the river...

She had been sitting there on the big rock since the dawn hours. Gone were those days on which she would come with her friend, Thabile, to this very rock. They would talk, laugh and gossip about anything with no care in the world, this day she was alone. Tears had not stopped flowing down her cheeks. She felt defeated by everything and everyone, love, marriage, friends, family, fate, the world and its people, she felt defeated by life altogether. Mandulo was not really a person of religion, she didn't go to church but she believed that God existed. She hadn't experienced the feeling of going to church with her mother, her mother was a drunkard and spent most of her life in taverns, shebeens or nightclubs. At that very moment Mandulo decided to pray, "Father, Lord, I'm sorry I'm not going to kneel down because there are dewdrops in the grass since it is still morning. God, I need you to tell me who's my father, I've spent the whole 27 years of my life without him and..." Tears got the better of her before she could continue, she allowed them to flow, she cried out loud. "Father, I need to know why my friend, Thabile, decided to take her own life. My marriage is falling apart, hold my hand. Everybody says you are a Man of Your word and I desperately need your help, Dear Father in Heaven. Amen." As soon as she opened her eyes she felt as though a burden was lifted off her shoulders.

It was Monday. Two days ago, news had reached her ears that her friend Thabile had committed suicide. It was believed that Thabile had thrown herself out of the window of the 9th floor in a flat she rented and lived in, somewhere in Durban. Nobody knew the reason behind it and nobody seemed to care, not even her family or the police, even Bonani didn't want to talk about Thabile's death. Mandulo was not a person with friends, ever since she was in grade two. She had been friendless almost her whole life until she recently met Thabile. When she was in grade two, she told a girl she regarded as a friend that she didn't know her father. The next day during break time the whole class, including that girl, was laughing at her about the fact that she was fatherless. That really got to her, and from there onwards she never liked friends. Besides, along her journey of life, she would meet people who would knock at the door of her life and wait for her to open. They would introduce themselves and occupy a certain seat in her life and a certain space in her heart, she would get attached to them. Then one day she would wake up to realize that they were gone, that they'd packed all their belongings and left, without saying goodbye, and leaving the door open. That had really hurt

Mandulo in the past, so she no longer believed in friends. Mandulo had known Thabile for only three months but it felt like she had known her for her whole life. She was different. They even made promises that they would never exit each other's lives. Thabile was more like a sister than a friend, but like all the others, she left without saying goodbye, leaving the door open. Mandulo was struck by great anguish in her heart, thinking about all that made her feel as though she would die. She looked at the big river which was nearby. The river was quiet but one could tell from a distance that it was desperate to tell its own stories. It was dark and looked deep, scary. A person would die right there if they happened to find themselves in it, Mandulo thought.

After a long stare at the river, she felt uneasy and decided to go back home, her husband must be wondering where she was, she thought. Bonani had managed to win both Mandulo's heart and trust. She was a Leo, so she had difficulty when it came to trusting anybody. They had been married for four years now and they were happy, if one may use that word. Mandulo loved Bonani with her soul, in the whole world she believed that he was the only person who had shown love and affection towards her, in the whole world she only trusted him. When they met, Mandulo was very fragile, she'd had her heart broken by almost every man who had once told her he loved her. Bonani spoke with his actions and she fell deeply for him. Bonani loved Mandulo and he had proven that quite a lot of times, from the time his mother had found out she never knew her father before and called her a fatherless hen, to the time when she found out that Mandulo was raped when she was 11 years old by a neighbour so she couldn't conceive. She was diagnosed with Pelvic Inflammatory Disease (PID) which caused her to become infertile, and his mother called her an infertile cow. Bonani stuck with her and protected her in every way he could. He had promised that he'd never hurt her and in the four years they had been married, he had kept all his promises. Mandulo felt bad when she thought about the fact that she could not give Bonani an heir but at least he understood and they agreed that they would adopt two children. A smile appeared on her face when she thought about Bonani. She remembered that she was about to leave, so she stood up and went back home.

When she arrived, it was not as quiet as usual. At the gate Mandulo was passed by Uncle Solomon's car, he greeted her briefly without even looking at her and went on with his journey. Usually, he would crack a joke or two, but not on that Monday and it was still morning, so something important was going on, Mandulo thought. Uncle Solomon was an elder of the Kheswa family, he was the only male person related to Bonani. They all respected him, even Bonani's mother, Ma Agnes, who seemed to have no respect for anyone. His word was the final one. Seeing his car, Mandulo's suspicions grew bigger, the old man never visited for just another cup of tea, something huge was going on. She went on to the dining room, then to the kitchen. "Aunty" had already arrived, that was evidence enough that it was Monday, she only came on Mondays and Thursdays. Seeing Mandulo, she disappeared to one of the bedrooms, leaving the dishes she was about to wash in the sink. This worried Mandulo. Aunty loved her and she treated her as her own daughter, the feeling was mutual. Everyone called her "Aunty" but Mandulo referred to her as "Ma". They always spoke using whatever chance they got and what Aunty had done worried Mandulo. Instead of going to their bedroom, Mandulo decided to go check up on Aunty. She found her in Ma Agnes' bedroom, on the chair next to the double bed. Aunty was just sitting there with a magazine she tried so hard to focus on. Mandulo came and sat on the bed across her, she didn't utter a word, she waited for her to speak first. Aunty was not prepared to say anything so it was up to Mandulo to break the ice.

"You know you can talk to me about anything Ma, I'll always be there for you," she started. "I'm so sorry my child," she could not continue, how was she supposed to tell Mandulo that very soon she could lose her husband to some other woman? "They are planning on taking another wife for Bonani, very soon. I'm really..." before she could finish Mandulo was gone. Mandulo was raped at age eleven by a neighbour since her mother had always been a drunkard. Every time her mother left her alone, that man got his chance. It took her time to gain enough courage to tell her mother, who went literally crazy after hearing the news. Indeed, Williness was a drunkard and she was not perfect but she would die for her daughter. She loved Mandulo and would do anything to make her happy. She made sure that the man never bothered her daughter again, she visited him for the night to have a beer with him, then the next morning he had died of food poisoning.

She was eleven years old when everything happened and 16 years had passed but she still remembered everything, that man destroyed her. Shortly after his death, Mandulo was diagnosed with PID and a few weeks later the doctor told her mother, in her presence that she was never going to have children for as long she lived. She and Bonani had agreed that they were going to adopt two children when the time was right. But Mandulo knew that this was going to happen, she knew that someday Bonani was going to be forced to take another wife "who would be able to bear him children," with Ma Agnes there, she just knew it. That woman simply hated her and she had long accepted it, but this was too much. She was not ready, that's if she was ever going to be ready to see her husband leaving her for another woman.

Mandulo was standing next to the gate, she didn't know whether to go to her mother or to go confront Bonani about what was happening. At least she knew her mother loved her and would always be there, but her pride would not allow her to go there, not after the last conversation they had had. It was World War Three of words, they were both in a state and hurting. "Mother, is my father still alive?" she had asked.

"Why does it matter Mandulo? Your father is absent in your life and it is time you accepted that you do not need him. Now focus on yourself and your marriage." That was always the reply to almost all Mandulo's questions about her father and it frustrated her.

"Every time I ask you about him, that is your answer, your question! Yes, it does matter, Mother, the man is my father. Maybe I would never have been raped if he had been there. He would have protected me and would not have gone to drink alcohol in the taverns leaving me with that man. My father would have protected my mother! Unlike you, maybe he loves me that much. As I am talking to you now I can't even bear children for my husband because you failed to protect me, and then you tell me to focus on my marriage? What do you know about marriages? You have failed, dismally, as a mother. You are no mother, to me you are as good as dead. I am motherless and I have accepted it." Her plan was to say these words and leave but her mother held her hand and looked her in the eye, for what seemed like five minutes, she didn't say a word.

Mandulo's mother drank a lot since she was a teenager. She got her name Williness from her drinking friends. Her surname was Williams and all her friends usually called her by it. The surname changed from Willy, to Willow and all sorts of names until they ended up calling her Williness. Williness loved Mandulo with her soul, she would jump in front of a moving train just to save her. When she heard years ago that a man had been raping her, she was deeply hurt. A part of her felt guilty because she always thought of how she could not protect her only daughter.

Through those years she had been trying to quit drinking because of what happened. What Mandulo did not know was that her mother, not disclosing any information to her was because she was trying to protect her from emotional hurt at that time. Mandulo's father was a man Williness had met when she had gone to a nightclub one night when she was just a young woman. He was the councillor of that place and everyone thought of him as a good man. He liked Williness and they slept together that very night after he had spiked her drink, without even using protection. In the morning that followed Williness found herself in a hotel, alone. He had left a note saying he had gone back to his life, with his cell number and a R200 note which he had written was for transport. After realizing that she was pregnant, Williness told him. He was so angry, he told her of his reputation, his wife, his family and his people. He then told Williness to abort the baby, and told her if she didn't he was going to kill her. Williness had always loved babies and so she was not about to kill her own baby, her blood and flesh, because a man had instructed her to. She ran from Cape Town and went to live with her Aunt in Durban. Her baby came first.

So, when Williness heard her daughter speaking like that, her heart broke. She didn't know how to tell her that her own father never loved her, that he wanted her aborted and threatened to kill her if she didn't.

"I've always been there Mandulo, when Aunt kicked me out I built us a home from the peanuts I earned. It has always been the two of us. I have always put you first," she said. And Williness was right, she had always put her daughter first.

She worked at the Municipality when she arrived at her Aunt's and the woman didn't treat them in a very good way, and when she tried to talk to her, she kicked them out. She was even trying to quit drinking alcohol so that Mandulo would be happy. "You are not perfect, my child. You have made your own mistakes and I have always been there. I'm not going to remind you of them, what I will remind you of though is the fact that I have never in my life disowned you as my daughter." She didn't say anything after that but within a few minutes, she was in her bedroom with a beer in her hands. She was hurt, even forgot that she had promised herself that she was never going to drink in her life. Mandulo was left there, she was crying. All she ever wanted was the truth about her father and she ended up hurting her mother, and now she couldn't go to her because of everything that had happened on that day, because of the last conversation they had had.

After thinking about all that, Mandulo decided not to go to her mother, instead, she went to her husband. When she arrived in their bedroom, Bonani was sitting on their bed on the far end as though there was no enough space. Mandulo sat next to him. Bonani's eyes were red and glassy. He then held Mandulo's hand, for a long time nobody spoke and they didn't look at each other. Mandulo could not hold it all in now, she cried out loudly.

"Will you marry her Bonani? Whoever this woman is, will you marry her?" Bonani looked at this creature. Mandulo was exquisite, dark in complexion, and there was something about her eyes, she had the most beautiful bright brown eyes, her lips were thick and pink. She had an afro.

"I love you," he finally replied.

"Will you marry her Bonani? Aren't we going to adopt anymore?" Bonani did not reply and that was all the answer Mandulo needed. So, she was going to be kept away from the love of her life because she could not give him children. Mandulo grew up fatherless, along the journey of her life some man raped her, she had no friends, and she had never trusted anyone except for Bonani. A few months ago, she had met Thabile, a friend she was prepared to trust but she left her. Bonani was the only person she trusted, the only person who had never left her. She had always been looking forward to being happy with him. She just wanted to know what people meant when they said they are happy, she just wanted to know what happiness felt like, but she was about to lose her ticket to happiness. Still crying, she stood up and was determined to go and apologize to her mother. She just wanted her hug. She left Bonani still seated on the bed. A part of him wanted to follow Mandulo but he decided against that, he decided to give her space.

When Mandulo arrived at her mother's house, she was literally running. Luckily her mother was there, cleaning the yard. She was really trying to be a better person, Williness had even stopped drinking during the day, instead of doing chores around the house. Mandulo ran and hugged her mother, she reluctantly returned the hug. "He is going to leave me for another woman, Mother. My husband is marrying someone

86

else." She let it all out and cried out loud. "I can't give him children, Mother!"

Williness held her daughter tightly in her arms, she would let her go once she had calmed down a little. After some time, she held Mandulo on her waist and they went inside the house. She had cooked pap and beef, Mandulo's favourite. When Williness realized that her daughter was not eating, she started feeding her, nobody spoke. After she was done eating, Williness made her a strong black tea.

"Here, it will help you, my child." They were both aware of what they were supposed to talk about. "I don't know where is he. He never loved you, Mandulo, he hated you the moment he heard I was pregnant and threatened that he was going to kill me if I did not abort. He cared about his wife and reputation more."

Mandulo could not stop the tears, it was better when she didn't know the truth after all. So, her mother slept with a married man who then threatened to kill her if she didn't abort their child. What kind of crime had she committed that she had to be killed while she was still in her mother's womb? She kept quiet while her mother told the whole story like a tale. Life had hated her since the very beginning.

When Mandulo left, Bonani started to cry, for the very first time since his father died when he was fourteen years old. He had diabetes and it got the better of him. He died after years of pain and suffering, leaving Ma Agnes to be labelled as a widow. The day Bonani visited him was the same day he died, his right leg had already been amputated.

"You are a man now Bonani, it's time you acted like one my boy because I'm no longer going to be there."

Those were his last words and they had always occupied a certain space in both Bonani's heart and mind. Bonani did not cry, not even in the old man's funeral, he regarded crying as something a real man should not do, and from that very day, he had never shed any tear. This day was different though, he cried, hysterically. He had broken the promise he had made four years earlier to Mandulo. Indeed, Bonani had no problem with the fact that Mandulo could not conceive, they were going to adopt. He had taught himself to love her wholeheartedly which is why he did not want another wife and had made his elders fully understand that, but what he had done was going to kill Mandulo...

His cellphone rang, it was Uncle Solomon. "Have you told your wife?" Bonani did not reply, "Do that before the police do. I'll call you later." Bonani did not want to hurt Mandulo, not after everything that had happened to her. He had failed as a husband. He had failed to give Mandulo the happiness she deserved but had never had, the happiness she had always longed for. The thought, again made him cry.

After the conversation they had, Mandulo and her mother, she just went straight to bed early. She didn't eat or bathe, she was not hungry and she felt that there was no need for her to bathe since even the love of her life was soon going to leave her. When her mother went to check up on her, the room was locked and she kept quiet when she shouted her name. She only replied, lying, to say she's been sleeping when her mother threatened to kick the door down. A lot of things were going on in her mind, she just wished that there at least was a way to end the pain, once and for all. She was not ready to face the world, she felt worthless. The man, who was supposed to be her first love, hated her before he even saw and met her and she didn't know where he was, she didn't even care. She closed her eyes and prayed that sleep was going to come and rescue her from reality, wishing to never wake up.

Around 01:00 am, Mandulo was not asleep, she was thinking about her wedding day, it was a surprise wedding. She was 23 years old then, Bonani was 26 years old. They had been dating for only a year but they both felt it was time. They would talk about how they wanted their wedding to be like and Mandulo could not wait to be pronounced as Mrs. Bonani Kheswa. She always made it clear that she didn't want many people at their wedding, more especially since she had no friends. She was at her home when her mother came and requested her to accompany her to Town for a "few things". She didn't ask too many questions and they went. She was confused when her mother took her to a big hall which she was sure was a church because it had a big cross on its rooftop. The moment they got inside, music started and there was a red carpet on which they went until they reached the aisle where Bonani took her hand from her mother and they faced the Pastor. She cried and could not believe what was happening. She laughed thinking about the dress she was wearing on that day and how embarrassed she was. They both didn't have too many friends, Mandulo had not even one. Bonani had two, who were his colleagues so he invited only them as friends. Their marriage was just a small ceremony, as she had always wished and she was happy with that. It was them, their mothers, Uncle Solomon, Bonani's friends and the Pastor. Bonani was so handsome, and she had always wondered why he chose her where he could have any girl in the world. By sunset that day, she was somebody's wife. If only life... Mandulo was taken back to the real world by her cell phone ringing, the time was 02:12 am, it was Bonani.

"Wife," he said. He usually called her like that and she would blush and smile but not on that day, things were different, she didn't reply and waited for him to continue. "I am not going to marry anyone else Mandulo, I promise. My family wanted me to marry…" he suddenly stopped.

"I am lost Bonani. What is going on? You know how I feel about you. You do know just how much I love you. You promised we were going to be happy and you know how much I am looking forward to our happily ever after," her voice was betraying her. Bonani could hear that she was now crying, that alone broke his heart. The last thing he had ever wanted in his whole life was to hurt Mandulo.

"I thank you for loving me Mandulo and I love you too sweetheart. Please do not cry, I won't leave you for someone else, but we do need to talk." Bonani knew that she was fragile, he knew that life had betrayed her countless times and now all her hope was in him. Hearing her cry, and not being able to hold her in his arms, and make sure she felt protected, and assure her that it all was going to be fine like he always did, it all broke him. "I'll come and fetch you, first thing in the morning. For now, please go to sleep, you need to rest. I love you." He just had to drop the call after he had said that, otherwise Mandulo was going to hear him cry. She wiped the tears and again closed her eyes, she desperately wanted to fall asleep, she did.

In the morning, Mandulo and Williness were woken up by a car pulling up in the yard. Mandulo walked out of the house and said goodbye to her mother, who gave her a very warm kiss on the lips and a very tight hug, even Mandulo felt uncomfortable. Bonani got out of the car to open the door for her and he kissed her on the forehead and got back inside. On their way, nobody spoke.

When they arrived, before they went out Bonani held Mandulo's hand and kissed it, "I love you," he then said and went out to open the door for her. Aunty was not there, Bonani had given her a week off, no reason. They went to sit at the kitchen table and Bonani prepared cereal for both. Neither of them was hungry and neither ate.

"Mandulo, I'm sorry," he said. Before she could say anything, Uncle Solomon and Ma Agnes came inside and sat on the empty chairs, joining the two at the table. They didn't say anything. "I had an affair, Mandulo, I slept with your friend Thabile and she fell pregnant." Mandulo could not feel her body, she felt numb. She did not want to hear anything else but when she tried to stand up and leave, her legs betrayed her, they felt weak as though the body they were carrying was too heavy. Yes, she wanted to say something but the words just couldn't come out. Her eyes felt dark and the only thing she could see was a black cloud. Tears could not come out, they were only glistering in her eyes. She remained seated on her chair and said nothing.

"Ma and Uncle wanted me to marry her. I made a promise that I would never hurt you Mandulo, so I could not, I refused. On Friday last week, I went to her flat. We were talking on the balcony and we argued because she wanted me to marry her or she was going to abort our child and tell the whole world about it if I didn't. She slapped me in the face and said a lot of other things," Bonani was crying. How was he supposed to say all the things Thabile had said about Mandulo, to her? A part of him wanted to lie but the least he would do was to tell the whole truth to Mandulo.

"She said you could not give me an heir I deserved so she should be the one I marry since she was going to do something you could not be able to. That is not an excuse but the things she said made me lose it. I did not mean to hurt her but I just saw her there, I had pushed her Mandulo. I killed Thabile, both her and my child." Ma Agnes got up from her chair and went to sit on the couch in the dining room. She put her hands on her thighs and her head on them and she screamed uncontrollably like a madwoman. Uncle Solomon sat there and stared into space. Bonani could not bear seeing the tears of an old man, he could not look at Mandulo either so he went outside to his car. He drove with no specific destination.

Even though her body felt heavy, Mandulo felt empty. She was not necessarily sad nor happy, or disappointed, she was empty and that was worse. She managed to stand up and slowly went to their bedroom, very careful not to fall, leaving Uncle Solomon glued on his chair. She took her cellphone in her skirt pocket and wrote a message to Williness, "I love you, Mother." She switched it off before she could get a reply. She then decided to pray, "Dear Father in Heaven, I'm sorry for what I am about to do, but please, Oh Lord, give me the strength, the energy and the power. Amen" She went and passed her mother-in-law in the dining room, who was still screaming. She opened the door and continued as though nothing was wrong.

In the yard, she met three police, two men and one woman. "Greetings Mem, I believe you are the young Mrs. Kheswa," one said. She didn't stop nor reply.

The other policeman continued, "There was an accident just down the road and your husband, Bonani Kheswa, was there. He was badly hurt so he was taken to hospital..." She didn't hear what he said after that. Mandulo. She started to run,

92

literally. She ran until she reached the big rock. All the memories started to play in her mind like a film. Thabile was just like the others. She had made a promise to herself that she was not going to trust anyone in her life but she trusted her, she trusted Bonani. She wished that he would wake up where ever hospital he was at. She thought of how she was looking forward to being happy, with the very man who had broken her in every way possible. She thought of her father, of that girl she was friends with in Grade Two, she thought of the man who raped her when she was just a 11-year-old girl, she thought of the hatred Ma Agnes had for her, she thought of Thabile, and Bonani. She thought of her mother, she was always there, but if only she agreed to abort her before she even came to this world which hated her before it even knew her, this world and its people. Her wish ever since she was a young girl, was to be happy. All she ever wanted was happiness. She then looked at the big river which was nearby, she closed her eyes and jumped into it. Her wish, never to wake up, was granted. She hoped that, wherever she was going, she was going to find happiness.

ABOUT THE AUTHOR

Mandisa Hadebe was born in 1999 December, on the 23rd in Port Shepstone, in a small village of KwaNdelu in Hibberdene. She values respect more than anything. Respect for herself, for all mankind, planet Earth, and Mother Nature. She believes in prayer more than anything. Growing up, she had always loved reading and playing netball in her primary school years.

Following an incident, she was unable to play netball or any other physical sports so she took up chess. She has always loved reading and writing pieces of literature, which she had hoped that she'd publish one day. Reading the many books, she has read has inspired and encouraged her to publish her own one day.

Flames of the Bare Brown Pastures is her first book. She has always hated fantasy and loved reality, as real as it is and as sour and distasteful as it may be sometimes. Oh, and she is not a believer in happy endings, as she believes that such do not exist.

As long as it's happy, then it's not an ending...

www.ingramcontent.com/pod-product-compliance
Lightning Source LLC
Chambersburg PA
CBHW050905180626

46814CB00007B/2910